Fiercely independent Belle Andrews can't quite believe where her life has ended up. Belle and Tash always thought they'd have three children, but after nineteen years and two children together, Tash walked out on her and Belle doesn't want her heart broken ever again.

Now, two years later, they've established a positive co-parenting relationship, and having moved on with their lives, both agree they have no need for the embryos they created together.

Georgia Reid has been trying, unsuccessfully, to get pregnant for many years now. She's about to give up trying and move on. Her doctor told her that her only hope now is a donor embryo.

Belle expects her embryos are the perfect solution, but she soon learns Australian legislation mandates she can only donate to someone she's in a relationship with.

Belle might have given up on love, but can she pretend to be in love to give someone their dream? And can Georgia pretend to be in a relationship with a woman to get the end result she's always dreamt of?

BABY STEPS

GEMMA JOHNS

A NineStar Press Publication
www.ninestarpress.com

Baby Steps

© 2023 Gemma Johns
Cover Art © 2023 Jaycee DeLorenzo

First Edition, March 2023

ISBN: 978-1-64890-625-1

Also available in eBook, ISBN: 978-1-64890-624-4

CONTENT WARNING:
This book contains sexually explicit content, which may only be suitable for mature readers. Depictions of infertility.

To my six children. You inspire me!

Chapter One

"I THOUGHT TASH had the girls tonight?" Nikki asked quietly so that Cora and Ada wouldn't hear her.

Belle shook her head. "We did a swap. She had something on tonight, probably with her new girlfriend." Belle knew she was reinforcing what her best friend Nikki already knew—Belle had well and truly moved on from her nineteen-year relationship.

"She's really got a new girl?"

Belle rolled her eyes. "Emily, I think she said. I don't know. It surprised me, because she was so full on with

Amanda. I thought they were it. But five minutes after their split, there was a bunch of dates with random women, and now there's Emily. I really don't care; it's none of my business, except for the girls."

Nikki instinctively looked toward the other room, where Belle's daughters were going crazy, running and jumping. "What do you mean, except for the girls?"

"You know." Belle followed Nikki's gaze. "As long as they're okay, constantly meeting new women in their other mum's life. Must be hard."

"Well, it's not really constant. Hopefully she'll stay with this one. She was with Amanda for, what? Two years?"

Belle nodded. "Depends who you listen to, but about that. But that's half of Ada's life. It just feels like a lot of change. Anyway, it's irrelevant to me, and leaves me to date whomever I want."

Nikki sarcastically stated, "Which you really take advantage of."

The truth was, Belle had no real desire to date, and although she and Tash had split up over two years ago now, Belle had spent her time focusing on the children. She couldn't say that Tash didn't focus on the girls, though. Belle and Tash were fortunate that they managed to co-parent so well together, with very little tension between the two of them. Belle would be lying to say it had always been easy. In the early days, her heart broke every time she dropped the children to Tash. Seeing Tash and Amanda playing happy families just months after her relationship with Tash had ended nearly destroyed her. But, with time and perspective, Belle felt more and more comfortable and sometimes found herself even confiding in Tash at the end of a hard day.

Nikki picked up her plate and empty coffee mug and walked to the sink. "I was going to suggest a movie tonight, because I thought you were footloose and fancy free."

"Why don't we watch a movie on Netflix?" Belle asked, and Nikki screwed up her face.

"I suppose. Chances are I've seen it."

Belle knew it was true. Nikki practically lived at the cinema.

*

THE NEXT MORNING, Belle stretched and rolled over in bed. She looked at her clock and was surprised to see it was after 9:00 a.m. Noting the silence in the house, she wondered what the girls were up to. She raced downstairs and found them both sitting in the living room watching ABC Kids on TV. "Hey, babies," she said, and the kids looked up from the television and smiled.

"Hey, Mama." Ada jumped into her mother's arms and gave her cuddles.

"We've got to get you dressed and give you breakfast before Mummy comes to pick you up."

The girls grinned.

"I told Ada to let you sleep in," Cora said, looking pleased with herself.

"Thank you, Cora. That was lovely. But now we have less than an hour to get you all ready to go home to Mummy for the week." When she first became a parent, Belle wondered if she'd ever get more than three hours sleep in a row, let alone sleep in past 9:00 a.m. The past few months had seen her claiming back some much needed 'me' time, even when she had the girls. Now that Cora had turned five, she was really starting to show consideration for the feelings of her parents.

"How about I put some porridge on?" Belle asked. Ada looked excited, while Cora jokingly pretended she was about to puke. "And toast for you, young lady?" Cora nodded, grinning. While the porridge cooked, Belle ensured the girls got dressed and put their bags by the front door. She and Tash both kept individual wardrobes and toys for the girls at their own house—it made the most sense with their week-about schedule—however, the girls took a small backpack of "necessities" between houses. Necessities weren't toothbrushes or pyjamas—they were covered. To the girls, necessities were particular Barbie dolls, their Nintendo Switches, a specific book, or whatever else took their fancy at that particular time. Today, Belle knew that in addition to the usual necessities, Cora had packed the Harry Potter box set she'd started watching. She only hoped Tash wasn't concerned about the fear factor. Tash always seemed more worried about which shows and movies the girls watched than Belle did.

"Hey," Tash said when Belle opened the door a little

while later.

"Hey, yourself." Belle gave Tash a peck on the cheek. "Come in. Tell me everything."

Tash blushed a little and raised her eyebrows, clearly thinking of her date with Emily the night before.

Belle grinned, adding, "Well, you don't have to tell me *literally* everything."

Before Tash had a chance to divulge everything or nothing, Cora came bounding up to her. "Mum. How are you?"

Tash grinned and embraced Cora, quickly followed by an embrace with Ava. "Great, great. What are you girls up to?"

"We're doing play dough and watching TV," Cora exclaimed. "Ava hurt me, because she wanted the blue play dough."

After giving the girls a lecture on playing nicely together, Tash said, "Why don't you go and play some more, and Mama and I will have a coffee and chat?"

The girls, excited to have more time at Mama's house, raced off without question. Belle put the kettle on, and Tash pouted. "I don't want instant." She pointed to the coffee machine. "I want one of those pod coffees. The real thing."

"I forget I have that machine," Belle said. "I only use it when I have company."

"What am I, if I'm not company?" Tash asked pointedly. "Besides, you should drink that coffee more often."

"I know. I just don't think to."

"I bet you pay five fifty for a cup at the café near your office."

"I do," Belle confessed with a grin.

"I've started making a cup in my Keep Cup each morning," Tash stated proudly. "Sometimes I even make two, because the cup keeps it hot enough for my afternoon coffee. And then I'm saving ten dollars a day." Tash shrugged. "That's fifty a week."

"I can do the maths." Belle wondered why it mattered to Tash.

"Actually, the maths is what I wanted to talk to you about."

"You're seriously worried about my coffee habit? What's it to you?" Belle asked.

"No, I don't really care how much money you waste on coffee, though I do think you should get a Keep Cup. No, I wanted to talk about something else." She paused, and then looked away and said, "I got sent the embryo renewal letter."

Belle was silent and frowned at Tash. Both of them knew the letter came every April, and every April, they just renewed it, even since they had broken up. It hadn't been discussed before, so Belle didn't know why Tash was bringing it up. Surely it couldn't have anything to do with Emily at this early stage. Then again, Belle knew how quickly Tash worked when she started dating someone. Although it was a surprise, Belle instantly knew she wouldn't make any rash decisions on someone else's time pressure.

Finally, she spoke. "Okay?" was all she responded with. That, combined with the long pause, said enough to Tash.

"It seems silly to keep paying it, given we're really done for good. But then we have six siblings for our girls in there. Emily and I don't need them."

Belle had a wry smile, more in surprise than anything

else. "Emily and you? There's already decisions being made around that?"

Tash shrugged, and Belle became increasingly frustrated with her. For such a huge topic, Tash seemed flippant, which was so unlike her. "I don't know what will happen with Emily, but I sense a connection. Last night was amazing. She gets me."

"Like Amanda got you?" Belle raised an eyebrow. Tash and Amanda had worked together and become a couple very quickly after Tash's shock decision to end their relationship. Belle had thought that she and Tash would be together forever—she wouldn't have had children with Tash otherwise. They were as good as married. They'd been together since they were kids themselves, after all. Tash's decision to leave had truly shocked Belle, and deep down Belle believed that Amanda was behind the end of their relationship. Tash was a very practical, detail oriented, and rational woman, but there was a small part of Tash that wore her heart on her sleeve, a romantic at heart. The romantic side of her was at odds with her practical nature, but it was always what Belle had admired about her ex. Unfortunately, once she was so busy with pregnancy and then parenting small children, Tash had her needs met elsewhere — at least, that's how it was as far as Belle was concerned. Neither Tash nor Amanda had ever confirmed this.

Tash swallowed and finally responded. "Amanda and me. Well, we weren't right for one another. Deep down. She helped me to get over you, as I grieved the loss of us, but she was a rebound girl. Deep down, I need someone more like Emily."

Belle simply shook her head and busied herself finalising the coffee making. She couldn't believe what she was hearing and didn't trust herself to speak. After a moment, she handed the bright red mug to Tash and steered her to the table. "Anyway, how does Emily have anything to do with *our* embryos?" Belle felt her emotions rising up to the surface and noticed her voice was a little higher pitched than usual. She wanted to get that under control, to continue the conversation, but was afraid her emotions would cause the conversation to go off course.

"Emily has nothing to do with our embryos." Tash practically whispered the word *embryos*, glancing at the TV room the girls were in as she muttered it.

While Belle agreed, her emotions were getting the better of her and she was finding it hard to be as rational about this as Tash was. "So?" Belle wasn't going to make this easy for Tash in any way. She wanted Tash to spell it out.

"So, I was thinking. I mean there's no chance we'd ever get back together and have another baby, right?" Tash asked, clearly nervous.

There was no chance, but a long time ago, Belle had wanted exactly that. Tash and Belle. Belle and Tash. They'd been together since she was just fifteen years old, and they'd planned to have three children. Those frozen embryos represented Belle's broken dreams, even if Tash no longer felt that way. There was a part of her that would always want that third child, but she knew she couldn't do it alone. She remained silent.

"I'm happy if you want to have a third on your own. Emily and I are talking about it, actually."

Belle nearly spluttered her coffee everywhere, but she choked it back instead. "A third child? You're talking about having another child?"

Tash couldn't hide her smile. "Emily wants to have a baby. Can you believe it?"

Suddenly the blood rushed to Belle's head and she felt a little breathless. "Oh, you're asking me if you can *use* the embryos? You're not asking me to destroy them?"

"Oh, God, no," Tash said. "It doesn't seem appropriate. To use the embryos created from your eggs. Besides, Emily would want to carry."

Belle was instantly relieved. "So, you've got it all worked out? That was fast." Belle couldn't hide the sadness in her voice, and Tash knew her well enough to pick up on it.

She reached for Belle's hand and lightly touched it. "Well, it's early days, Annabelle. Early days." She smiled reassuringly at Belle. "But what are your plans? Do you still want to try for number three? I know you always wanted to."

Belle sipped her coffee and put her head back, glancing at the ceiling. "I'm single," she finally said, and looked down at the table.

"And you're a kick-ass single mum as it is."

Belle blushed in gratitude, but couldn't quite believe Tash would be the one having a third child, and she wouldn't.

"You could absolutely have a third and you'd do it amazingly."

"Work is so busy." It was true. Belle had really thrown herself into her career over the past two years and was loving it. "Every second week I work really long hours and try to have a bit more balance when I have the girls. I wouldn't have that as a sole parent of a third child. Plus, oh my gosh, those newborn days. Doing that alone..." Belle slowly shook her head, recalling how tough the newborn days had been for her. "It'd be too hard. But thank you for the compliment."

Tash firmly put her hand on the table. "Fair enough," she said, as if the case was closed and everyone was happy. "Then, what do we do with the embryos?"

"I was hoping to not do anything," Belle said firmly.

Tash grimaced a little. "It's a bit unfair to Emily, though, isn't it? And financially silly. But mostly it seems wrong to say to Emily that I have kids in the freezer with my ex-wife while she's maybe trying for a baby? It's just a bit… Well, it seems a little wacky." Tash at least looked a little embarrassed.

Belle tried to not let her anger show. She didn't particularly care about Emily's feelings about this. "I need time to think. Can we leave it this year, as is?"

"Can you pay the bill, though?" Tash asked. "Take over the financial side, 100 per cent?" Tash sounded a little whiney.

"Yeah. Sure. The money isn't the issue for me, so if that's the concern for you, I'll pay the account."

"You can then make any calls you want with them. Basically, I'll wipe my hands of the embryos, and they'll become yours."

Belle couldn't really believe Tash felt this way and tried to think it all through quickly. "I'd need your permission, in terms of the clinic. They're not my embryos; they're *our* embryos. So you'd effectively be signing off on them." Belle needed to know that Tash understood.

"I'm not going anywhere, so just let me know when you decide. I'll scan you the letter today, and you can pay it, and then buy yourself some time. I know it's tough," Tash acknowledged.

"Is it tough for you?" Belle asked, her forehead crinkling.

Tash was clearly confused and asked for clarification.

"You and Emily have a baby, and it's not connected to Cora and Ada genetically."

"Oh," Tash said. "That was the other thing I wanted to chat with you about. I think our donor is still donating. I wondered how you felt if Emily and I used the girls' sperm donor? Seems to make sense for the girls to have a half sibling, especially if you're not having another child." Tash then rushed to add, "If we go down the baby path, that is. It's still early days. Too early to make any plans like that."

Belle knew in her heart that Tash and Emily would proceed. She stayed silent for a moment as she thought it over and agreed it made sense for the children to be genetically connected with their new siblings. Although it broke her heart, she consented to Tash and Emily using the same donor.

Chapter Two

ONCE TASH AND the girls had left, Belle sat on the couch reeling from the discussion. She already had a headache forming from the stress. She called Nikki up and asked her for dinner.

"Okay. Maybe we can catch that movie?" Nikki asked, but Belle said no, she had to talk.

"Sounds big," Nikki said. "I'll meet you at La Dolce Vita at six?"

Belle spent the afternoon aimlessly pottering around the house and listlessly sitting on the couch. At around 5:00

p.m., she finally got dressed for dinner. Belle put a bright red top on with blue jeans and boots. She ran her fingers through her long brown hair, put a smear of lipstick on her lips, and marched out the door. She arrived at the restaurant at 5:30 p.m. and grabbed a table. She drank coffee while trying to read a novel but couldn't keep her mind on the story. Finally, Nikki breezed into the restaurant in a long, blue patterned dress.

"Oh, I like this," Belle said, gesturing at the dress. "It's new?"

Nikki smiled. "It is. I'm pleased it meets your approval, Ms Fashionista! I got it in the end-of-summer sales to meet Jason's parents. I'm taking advantage of the last few warm days to wear it."

"Oh, shit, that was today? Meeting Jason's parents?" Belle had been so preoccupied with her own drama she'd completely forgotten that Nikki was meeting her boyfriend's parents for a family lunch. "How did it go?"

"Really good. They seemed to really like me."

"How could they not?" Belle always joked with Nikki about her confidence.

"Well, yeah. How could they not?" Nikki smiled. "No, in all seriousness, they were friendly, happy, and lunch was good. I haven't scared Jason off."

"That's fabulous. Remember that time with Stefan? When you met his parents?"

Nikki and Belle had been friends since high school, so Nikki had been by Belle's side throughout her entire relationship with Tash, and Belle had been there for all the ups and downs of Nikki's relationships. Stefan's parents hadn't liked Nikki from day one of their short-lived relationship, because they still held a torch for Stefan's ex, Dora. Interestingly, Stefan ended up marrying Dora, they heard along the grapevine.

Nikki raised her eyebrows. "I think that goes down in history as the ultimate bad parents' reaction. I don't think any parents would ever be so bad to a new partner."

"You never know. But I'm pleased that Jason's parents loved you."

"So, the food and company is great, but what was with the urgent catch up? Sunday night, Jase and I were planning a night in watching TV and making mad passionate love to one another."

Belle cringed. "Okay, okay. Enough's enough." She laughed and threw a piece of garlic bread at her friend. "But I am sorry, I didn't even think. You were with me last night too."

"I know. Jason will think we have a thing."

Belle knew Nikki was joking. The idea was ludicrous. "Anyway, Tash came over today, and she wanted to talk about the embryos." Belle explained the whole thing—about Tash and Emily planning to have another child, about the donor, and finally, about Tash's plans with the embryos.

Nikki was clearly shocked. "Have you thought about a third child?" she asked tentatively.

"Of course I have. You know, when I was with Tash, it was all I wanted, to be honest. I thought that we'd be starting just around the time that Tash ended things. And then after we broke up, I spent so long focused on just being a mum that I figured one more wouldn't hurt. I wasn't dating, but I thought, well, at least I don't have to date to be a single mum. I can just get the embryo transferred, and boom. But I was worried it would have me so tied to Tash, by using our embryos. I was worried she wouldn't say I could. So I didn't do it."

"And now she's given you that on a platter?"

"She has…"

"What will you do?"

"It's like… It feels like…that ship's sailed. I feel like…there will always be a part of me that wondered what if, but I've now moved on. I think, anyway. My career is doing well; the girls are getting more independent. I know that sounds crazy, at five and four. But this morning I slept in until nine. Can I really go back to the baby days? Or maybe I can, but do I really want to? And full time, on my own, with no partner? I'd have to really want it to make such a drastic decision. I just don't know if I do anymore."

Nikki looked closely at her friend. "You know, I could help you. I could hang out with you. I could visit, babysit. I wouldn't be a co-parent, but I'd be there for you."

"Thank you. And I really appreciate it, but it's not the same as having someone there."

"Well, we could even move in together? It'd still be your child, but I could be on hand to help out any time."

"Which would be great, I'd love that, and I love you for offering, but what if you and Jason want to move in together some time? It's not fair on you to have you in wait with me so I can live out my dream. Plus, it'd be like a pseudo-relationship, and I can't do that to either of us."

"Back up, though—*dream*. You said, 'so I can live out my dream.' I really think you need to do it, Belle."

Belle looked into the distance as she thought about the advice Nikki was giving her. "I don't think I do. But I think I want to donate the embryos." The idea just popped into her head as they were talking, and it surprised Belle almost as much as it surprised Nikki.

"Oh. Wow," Nikki said, her surprise evident. "Have you thought about it all? Are you certain? And do you need to talk to Tash?"

"I don't think I need to talk to Tash. She said she's happy for me to make the call. But I need to think over the implications for the girls, I suppose. I guess I just need to spend some time mulling it over. Truth is, I haven't thought about it, really, until now."

"Maybe it's too soon to make any calls then."

Belle agreed. She knew she would absolutely pay the bill for the April renewal, giving her twelve months to make a decision, but she also knew she couldn't leave this hanging over her head for twelve months.

Belle and Nikki kept eating and laughing over silly chatter; then they parted ways, with Nikki excited to return to Jason's house, and Belle returning to her empty home. She'd left the TV on, something she often did as she went out, just for a bit of comfort when she returned home. She still didn't love arriving home to an empty house. And despite this, she actually enjoyed living alone, something she'd never done before, moving from her parents' house into a share house with Tash and eventually buying their first home together. It was like two worlds—one week, the girls filled the house, making it chaotic, and Belle wished for quiet. Then, when the girls were with Tash, she pined for their constant chatter. She tried to be happy with the present, but Belle was always wondering how she ended up here. When she'd met Tash, she'd thought it would be the two of them against the world, forever more.

Chapter Three

THE INCIDENT THAT got her and Tash together was possibly one of the most mortifying incidents in her life. Belle was at a school dance, watching all her friends trying to catch the eye of all the boys and dancing moves that raised even her own eyebrows. Belle went to the bathroom and was brushing down her clothes when Jenny, a girl from her science class, came out of the cubicle. They began talking and eventually walked out to a quiet garden area, still talking about the dance and all the girls fussing over the boys. Belle admitted she wasn't interested in the boys, and Jenny asked Belle if she was interested in girls. Belle had just come out to herself and wondered if Jenny was potentially interested. She'd confessed to Jenny that, yes, she was interested in girls—something she hadn't even told Nikki at that point. Jenny had looked horrified and responded, "I actually thought you would have said no to that. I've never known a lesbian before." To her credit, Jenny talked to Belle for a little longer, but after a few minutes, they returned to the dance and went their separate ways.

On Monday, however, the news had spread that Belle was a lesbian. Nikki was the one to break the news to Belle, confronting her in complete disbelief. At lunchtime, things got worse, when a group of girls taunted her and called her names. Belle had never been one to draw attention to herself and was mortified that her sexuality was being so publicly discussed while she was still coming to terms with it. She was angry with Jenny, but later discovered Jenny had only told one person and the rumour had spread like wildfire from there.

Tash, the school's vice captain, two grades above Belle, heard the commotion and strode over to the group of girls surrounding Belle.

"What's going on?" Tash asked. Many of the girls backed away, but a few remained and whispered to Tash that Belle was a lesbian. Belle was mortified and panicked that she was being dobbed into a school captain. She put her head into her hands, buying herself some time before she had to meet the eyes of the school leader. The older girl trying to sort things out.

When she finally looked up, she realised Tash had sent the girls on their way and sorted out all their drama. Belle was mortified. "I'm so sorry," she said. "I'm sorry you had to come and fix that, and I promise you I've never done anything lesbian and certainly never will while I'm at school."

Tash nodded, her blonde ponytail swishing. "None of my business," Tash said, matter-of-fact. "That's your business, and your business only."

Belle was still anxious, but gave her a small, grateful smile. "Thanks."

"I'm a little worried about you, though," Tash said, which surprised Belle. "That must have been really hard to experience."

Belle nodded awkwardly, finding herself opening up to this girl she had never talked to. "Well, I'm certainly not excited about coming to school again tomorrow, or, you know, the next two and a half years!"

"You'll be okay. Maybe it would be worth getting some counselling."

Belle raised her eyebrows. "I'm sure the nuns would love to hear about that." She knew she was blushing. "I'll be okay. I'm sure there are plenty of other gay girls at this school." Belle gestured around the playground.

"Oh, there are," Tash said with certainty.

When Belle and Tash told this story for the years to come, at various dinner parties or even just amongst themselves, as couples always do, Belle always wondered how she hadn't picked up Tash's loaded tone. The way Tash would eventually tell the story, this conversation was laden with flirtation and inuendo that Belle had totally missed; however, Belle was sure Tash had been just as anxious herself.

Over the next few weeks, the two of them became friends, starting with Tash taking Belle out for the occasional milkshake to talk things through. Tash had said to Belle that if she wasn't going to see a counsellor, they'd at least have a regular milkshake to chat. It wasn't until a few weeks later that Tash finally confessed to Belle that she, too, was gay. She had everything to lose, though, in her mind, and so no one knew—not her parents, nor any of her family members, and certainly not any of her classmates at school. As the school's vice captain, she didn't want to be the topic of discussion—she wanted a clean slate.

Furthermore, Tash was finishing school and heading into law school the following year—all going to plan that was, which for Tash always seemed to happen. For seventeen-year-old Tash, the stakes seemed too high, and so she wasn't going to do anything to jeopardise her future, or her image at her school. That was more important than her heart, she'd decided. She wouldn't ruin it on a whim. At least, that was the plan, but over numerous milkshake dates, eventually hanging out at one another's houses, and even the odd sleepover, Belle and Tash became so important to one another that it felt so natural when Tash embraced Belle one evening, and they finally shared their first kiss. It wasn't just their first kiss together; it was their first kiss *ever*.

Belle couldn't wipe the grin off her face for weeks. She couldn't believe that someone so pulled together and smart was interested in her. She couldn't believe that Natasha Maree Evans was her girlfriend! Tash seemed just as happy, if not a little more low-key about things. They were both delighted, and the two of them spent every minute possible together. With Tash's permission, they eventually told Nikki who was relieved that Belle hadn't just found a best friend to replace her.

Despite taking the plunge on a relationship, Tash's plan still did come to fruition, and she went to university to study law, while Belle finished high school. Eventually Belle joined Tash at university, studying events management and fashion, and they moved into a large share house with Nikki and two guys from Tash's law school. That house had a bit of a rotating door, though, with people coming and going — Tash, Belle, and Nikki always remaining.

Tash graduated a year before Belle and became a graduate lawyer at some large firm in the city. Belle worked all through her studies in fashion stores and eventually got a full-time job coordinating various fashion parades and managing a small chain of stores. When Belle got her full-time job, Tash and Belle rented an apartment together—their first ever "couple" home. A year later they bought a different apartment in the same block—their first real home—and celebrated by throwing a civilised housewarming party, feeling very grown up.

By the time she was twenty-four, Belle was employed full time as an event manager for a slightly larger chain, and Tash, twenty-six, was exhausted by her busy law career. One night, Tash came home at eight, scoffed down the dinner that Belle had cooked, and said, "Let's go and live in London!"

"London?" Belle had asked. This seemed so out of the blue.

"Why not? Every Australian eventually spends time in the UK. I'm nearly thirty. Life is passing me by! And look, I get home at eight o'clock!"

Belle pondered the idea. International experience would be beneficial for someone working in fashion, and so they rented their apartment out, packed their things in storage, and said farewell to their families and friends.

Belle and Tash had a ball in London, and eventually New York when the company Belle was working for expanded over there. The experience was excellent for her career but probably made little difference to Tash's. Tash didn't care about that—she was hardworking but seemed a little burnt out. She was no longer particularly ambitious. Her legal career had jaded her a bit and she just wanted to do the "right thing," rather than necessarily work harder to succeed quickly. Belle, on the other hand, was feeling inspired in her field, so climbing the ladder was now Belle's goal. By then, Tash had caught the travel bug and was thrilled to be able to spend her weekends flitting off to Ireland or the Netherlands when they were in London, and to DC or even Canada when they were in New York. They didn't go home once in their five years overseas—something which wasn't particularly popular with their families—but Belle and Tash were having far too much fun and enjoying one another's company so much that they never felt lonely.

They managed to talk to their families through Skype

and WhatsApp regularly enough, and at the end of their five years, they reluctantly packed up to return home to their apartment. Tash in particular felt down about returning home but was also ready to leave the US. She needed something to look forward to, she had said. Belle suggested attending concerts, weekends away, or maybe planning a cruise, but nothing seemed to hit the spot for Tash.

Suddenly, Tash suggested they start a family. Again, Belle was surprised, but she'd learnt enough about Tash over the years to understand that Tash did get a bit directionless and flat if she didn't have something energising her. Besides, they'd been together such a long time, and Belle was twenty-nine and Tash had just turned thirty-one. Maybe it *was* time to settle down, back home in Australia, and start a family. They agreed that their apartment wouldn't be suitable, so made a decision to buy a house when they got back to Brisbane.

They returned home to the excited embraces from their families, and moved in with Tash's family for a few months while house hunting. They finally purchased a five-bedroom, two-bathroom house, that stretched them to their limits, but left just enough to pay for the fertility treatment they planned. Tash had done all the sums—as spontaneous as she was to make decisions, she was the planner of the two of them and left nothing to chance. Through all of this, they'd never discussed who would carry the baby, and Belle assumed that Tash might want to, given her age, but when they finally got around to the conversation, Tash said she wanted a "mini Belle" and would prefer to not carry herself. Belle was secretly delighted, and they commenced the series of required medical appointments.

On the day of the egg retrieval, the fertility specialist had said he was hoping to get ten eggs, based on the scans. When Belle woke from the sedation and saw the number fifteen written on her hand, she was even more delighted. Fifteen eggs gave them many more chances. With fifteen eggs, they'd definitely get a baby, Belle thought.

The fertility specialists worked their magic, mixing the fifteen eggs with the magic sperm the couple had shipped in from the clinic. Tash had spent many nights looking for a donor. It was Belle's request that Tash select the donor, since they were using Belle's eggs. Eventually, Tash provided

Belle with the donor codes of three men, and Belle had to make the final decision out of the three. She opted for a blonde-haired, blue-eyed donor, to match Tash's appearance, and he happened to be a law student, selected for obvious reasons. Tash was thrilled with Belle's choice, and the two of them proceeded, never once imagining that life wouldn't work out happy ever after—at least, as far as Belle was concerned.

First, only thirteen eggs fertilised, and the clinic told them this was very good news. Belle wasn't worried; it only took one embryo to produce a baby.

The first cycle didn't work, though.

Belle and Tash came crashing down. Everything pretty much went to plan for the two of them, and so to have a hiccup caused them so much grief. Belle tried to be optimistic. They'd try again two months later. Two months later, though, and they got yet another phone call telling them that Belle wasn't pregnant. A lot of tears, a lot of emotions, a lot of stress and tension. They tried three more times. Belle suggested they try to get Tash pregnant, but Tash asked Belle to try six goes. The IVF was causing Belle to get so emotional, which was unlike her, and she was resenting Tash getting on with her normal life. Eventually on the sixth attempt, the doctor suggested they transfer two embryos. Somehow that worked. They finally received the phone call that had them in tears of joy, rather than tears of sadness. Pregnant!

Belle and Tash celebrated and told their families and Nikki. They were simply thrilled, calculating the due date.

"I wonder if it's twins," Tash said excitedly. "I wonder if both embryos took." Belle was secretly relieved when the scan showed just one heartbeat.

The months passed, and the couple excitedly prepared the nursery, bought the pram, and discussed the various parenting books they read. When Cora arrived, kicking and screaming into the world, the new mums were absolutely in love and agreed they wanted another two children. Given how long it had taken for Belle to fall pregnant with Cora, Tash gently suggested that Belle should try again sooner rather than later, and Belle reluctantly agreed, even stopping breastfeeding early so that they could try again. They rushed back to the clinic to do a frozen embryo transfer to start the process for a sibling for Cora. This time they were shocked that it worked first go. Their babies would be just fifteen months apart. Belle was anxious, but Tash seemed excited and told Belle not to worry, which calmed Belle a little. They were a team, and they would manage.

But as the pregnancy progressed, Tash became anxious. Cora was waking often, and Belle and Tash were struggling with their sleepless nights. Their anxiety about coping with two small babies heightened. Suddenly both Belle and Tash were nervous and worrying, and that led to them snapping at one another, and generally not having much fun together. By the time Ada was born, Belle and Tash felt almost like strangers to one another, and they didn't know how to reclaim the incredibly close bond they'd once shared. Belle read relationship books and tried to implement strategies. They kept talking about how they may be able to reconnect, about ways to carve out some more *me* time and *couple* time, but over the months and weeks, Tash's *me* time apparently became *us* time for her and Amanda. By the time Belle felt she was coming through the fog of parenting two young babies and finally felt ready to take some time to get their careers and relationship back on track a little before completing their family with a third child, Tash had ended their nineteen-year relationship.

Belle was shocked. She hadn't seen it coming.

Nearly two decades as lovers, best friends, and partners in life—more than half their life, and two babies later—and their relationship was completely done. The end of their romance felt like the end of all of Belle's hopes and dreams. If she couldn't make it work with Tash, the love of her life, the person who knew her better than anyone, then she couldn't make it work with anyone else. The end of their romance somehow made it seem that all of their memories—of their five years travelling together, of all of the nights spent talking until the early hours of the morning, of all of their adventures, hopes, and dreams—had never happened. Their relationship was witness to hours and hours of conversations, dates, and adventures, and these stories would no longer grow old with them. Belle had never felt so lonely, and yet, she was the mother to two young children. She never really got a moment alone. *How can you be lonely when you're never alone?*

Belle didn't understand why Tash wasn't willing to try to fix things, especially after their amazing adventures together, and she persisted, trying to get them to see a counsellor or talk openly about what was going wrong. Belle sent Tash letters, text messages, and arranged catch ups, hoping that Tash would understand what they were saying goodbye to by ending things. Their future, and the life they'd imagined for their children, and eventually, perhaps, their grandchildren.

Finally, months after their relationship ended, Tash told Belle that she'd started dating Amanda. Belle wasn't stupid. She realised they'd started an affair before Tash had ended their relationship. No wonder Tash hadn't been willing to try. Belle was broken hearted, but somehow it helped her to know there was no chance. It was pointless to keep trying. It was Tash's choice. Everything had always been Tash's choice.

Belle spent the first year single trying to work out what Belle's choice was, without Tash's input. The trouble was, she didn't really know what she'd wanted. She'd started dating Tash when they were so young that everything Belle had done had been somehow influenced by Tash. Tash was taller, slimmer, smarter, prettier, older, and much more opinionated. Belle had always felt fortunate to have caught Tash's interest and happy to follow along with Tash's whims. She should have known Tash's interest would have been fleeting. She had worried about that in the early days, but over sleepovers and milkshakes, they'd seemed to establish such a strong bond that Belle, at least, thought what they had was forever.

Tash had been the leader in their relationship—from the pace of their relationship, to their decision to travel, to return, to have a baby, even which brands of products to buy; hell, she was even the leader in all the sexual adventures they'd shared. Though they'd moved to America for Belle's career, it was mostly because, by then, Tash was bored in the UK and felt that a change of scenery was what was needed. Perhaps Tash was always quickly bored, always looking for the next adventure. In the absence of study, career, travel, and IVF, her new adventures had become girls—Amanda first, and finally Amanda wasn't enough, and she'd moved on to a string of various women, and now Emily. In some ways Belle pitied her.

Now, Tash was making another choice. She was going to have a third baby, and she was giving away their embryos to Belle. Belle had never thought of the embryos as hers because despite being connected to her genetically they were *theirs*—Tash's and Belle's. They wouldn't have happened if it weren't for the two of them, and they wouldn't have happened without the donor Tash had carefully selected. The donor that Emily would now get pregnant by.

Belle was hurt, frustrated, and anxious about the future. She knew that opting not to have a third baby was going to be hard, particularly when she saw Cora and Ada's new sibling when Tash and Emily exchanged the girls back and forth. However, she was on track for another promotion and feeling especially inspired by her career. She didn't want to return to the baby days given she was now alone. On the spur of the moment, Belle had mentioned donating the embryos when she'd talked to Nikki, and the more she thought about it, the more it made sense. The clinic had told them that they could donate embryos to another family, to science, or discard them. Discarding them was simply out of the question to her. Perhaps it was Catholic guilt, but there was no way Belle could do that. Science or another family, therefore, were her only options. Without their donor, they wouldn't have Cora and Ada, so Belle thought donation to a family might make sense—a nice way to give back.

Chapter Four

BELLE WOKE UP on Monday morning and grabbed her gym bag. Her gym habit was a little haphazard—she only ever went the weeks she didn't have the girls, and even then, she wasn't always committed to rising early. If she allowed herself to put off until the evening, she never felt like going. This particular Monday, she jumped up, dressed in her leggings and T-shirt, and drove to the gym for a spin class. She loved cycle classes the most because she found she could switch off almost completely and just pump her legs, cycling her way through the sixty minutes. In contrast, dance classes or aerobics required so much concentration for her that they weren't a stress relief. Although Belle loved dancing, she felt awkward trying to follow the instructor's moves—something she didn't feel when she was hidden away on the back, corner bicycle.

After her workout, she went to the gym shower, then dressed in a vibrant red work dress, heels, and cardigan; she felt ready to face the day. The gym offered a basic breakfast as part of the membership—more motivation to go to the gym in the morning, rather than wait until after work. She sat with her bowl of muesli, topped with cereal, coupled with a glass of juice, and read the novel she was half-way through. Belle sighed happily. Although she never signed up to a life of fifty-fifty parenting, she had to admit, there were some perks to it. Having more *me* time than she'd had in a long time seemed like the bonus of a bad situation.

Through the day, her decision about the embryos was nagging at her. Although Belle had given herself up to a year to decide, she didn't want to live wondering. Instead, she wanted to decide what was the best decision. She knew she needed to know more. So, that evening, after making herself a chicken stir-fry and devouring it in front of the TV, Belle reached for her laptop and started to research embryo donation. She found a few Facebook groups, on which she lurked rather than participated. Some people who became parents through embryo donation seemed to be incredibly grateful for the gift they received, while others felt sad that they hadn't managed to conceive on their own. Then, there were the donor-conceived kids, now adults, who also seemed to fall into two categories—those incredibly grateful for both their donors and their parents, and those who resented that they'd been donor conceived and almost felt that a life as a donor-conceived child might have been worse than no life at all.

Belle had to admit to herself that these people in particular pulled at her heart strings, and she wondered if she was just better off donating to science. But, the stories of the grateful donor conceived kids and the very grateful recipient parents warmed her heart. As she scrolled through message after message while sipping a warm mug of hot chocolate, Belle had no idea what to think or what plan of action to take. Not for the first time, she was sad that Tash was planning to have a third child while Belle was effectively giving her wish for a third child away—donating her dream. Tash and Emily could be living this dream together. It made Belle really question why Tash had ended their relationship. Belle had often consoled herself, thinking perhaps Tash wasn't cut out for full time parenting, and it was easier to walk away when the going got tough. Perhaps Tash was attracted to the idea of raising their kids fifty-fifty so she got a break.

But now, she was embarking on full-time parenting with Emily—all going to plan, that is. Maybe it was Belle that had driven Tash away, not just the circumstances of their life. It was all too much to consider, and really saddened Belle. She had come to terms with the end of their relationship long ago, but the idea of a third child had always been her plan, and she couldn't help but resent that Tash and Emily would be living her dream.

Later in the week, after working too many hours to be healthy, Belle was looking forward to a relaxing weekend prior to getting the children back on Sunday. Normally the kid handover was done on a Friday night, after school and day care, but because of the swap the weekend prior, this week it would occur on the Sunday. Belle had to admit she was looking forward to having some time alone after such a long week. Maybe Sundays were a better day for handover, given both she and Tash tried to do more work in their child-free week. Still, she supposed that soon enough it wouldn't matter to Tash, once she had a third child. Her whole life would revolve around a baby's routine once again. Belle didn't envy that.

On Friday evening, she went for drinks with some people from work. It felt nice to let her hair down, and one of the advantages of being single and living alone was that she didn't have to answer to anyone. It wasn't that Belle was a party girl—it was just nice to go out and not watch the clock, to not have someone expecting her home, waiting for her. Belle led a fairly quiet life though, so drinks after work on a Friday night was about as exciting as it got. Occasionally she'd go out dancing with Nikki, but that tended to depend on Nikki's relationship status, and now that Nikki was happily coupled up again, Belle expected that would be off the cards. Belle did enjoy going to a gay nightclub every now and again, just to feel part of the scene, but so much had changed since she was young, and having coupled up in high school, she'd never really been part of the scene, anyway. These days, the clubs certainly made her feel old and boring. She loved to dance but felt old and frumpy on the dance floor. She hadn't even slept with anyone but Tash. She just wasn't a casual fling type of girl.

Just as much as she didn't want to chase women for anything casual, she also didn't want another relationship. Although Nikki and Belle's sister, Alex, regularly encouraged Belle to date online, any time Belle started to look, she lost interest pretty quickly. She simply didn't have the faith in relationships that she'd once had. Blind trust was not something she believed in anymore. She felt jaded and cranky with women, even though it was just Tash who'd hurt her. No, dating wasn't on the agenda. Belle had long ago decided it was best to just focus on work and the kids — and they kept her busy enough.

Chapter Five

ALTHOUGH SHE LOVED pottering around the house on a Saturday morning, Belle was pleased to be invited by Nikki to shop for jeans and have a late lunch. Belle threw her favourite jeans and red Converse shoes on, along with a red Henley top.

"Oh, I like those jeans," Nikki said as they kissed hello. "That's what I want—a pair of jeans that look equally good with sneakers or heels."

Belle was excited to help out. It had been too long since their last shopping trip. "I am happy to be your assistant, but whatever we do, do not let me leave with more jeans! I have a wardrobe bursting with them."

"It's a deal, providing you'll have lunch at Fasta Pasta." Belle rolled her eyes; she much preferred a café or something a bit more civilised than Fasta Pasta, but Nikki loved it, and Belle was happy enough to indulge her friend. In some ways it reminded them of their high school days, when they spent many hours dining at Sizzler or Fasta Pasta and gossiping about the other kids at school.

Ninety minutes later, Nikki and Belle had finished shopping for jeans and their tummies were grumbling.

"We're not going to Fasta Pasta," Belle joked. "The deal was you had to stop me buying jeans, and you didn't." Belle gestured to the black shopping bag in her hand. "In fact, you let me get two pairs. For someone working in fashion, I can't be constantly in jeans."

"Jeggings aren't jeans, and those ripped black jeans suited you so much. It would have been a crime to stop you. Besides, you're a grown woman—I could hardly stop you spending your cash on jeans that make your ass look so hot."

"Thanks. For that compliment, you can go to Fasta Pasta."

"Excellent," Nikki said, already leading the way.

*

AFTER THEY'D ORDERED their meals and the garlic bread and drinks had already arrived at their table, Nikki stopped joking with Belle and asked her how she was progressing on the embryo donation decision. Belle told her all about her research from the night before.

"Do you want to know the person you're donating to?" Nikki asked, her forehead creasing.

Belle sipped her drink as she thought. "Deep down, possibly. I wouldn't want to be a close contact, I don't think. I mean, if you wanted the embryos, of course, or if Alex did." Alexandra, Belle's sister, was childless by choice, so Belle thought it was probably a moot point. "But it wouldn't be bad to have some kind of connection with the person. Maybe. I don't know." The people on the sites she had researched had mixed thoughts about this. Some liked to just donate and never see or hear of it again, others liked to get regular photos, and some became an "aunty" or "uncle" of sorts. "Maybe photos would be cool. Gosh, it's so hard, I have no idea."

"But you're doing it?" Nikki asked.

"I think so—it seems to be the only thing that seems logical to me, personally. Destroying them isn't for me, so it's science, otherwise. And that's so important, but I'd love to help a family out." Belle didn't really mind what that family looked like—gay or straight, with or without kids already—she just wanted to help.

As the main meals arrived, Nikki finally asked the question that Belle hated, because there was no straight answer. "You definitely don't want a third?"

"You know, if things were different…"

"What if you meet someone?"

Belle knew that wasn't on the cards. "I'm not going to. I don't want another relationship."

"You're going to grow old alone?" Nikki raised an eyebrow.

"I have you; I have my friends, my family. I even have Tash, in some twisted way. And I have my kids. I'll never be alone."

"That's true, but sitting at home on a Saturday night, cuddled up with your partner, is different to having friends and family around." Belle considered this but remained silent, so Nikki continued. "I'm just saying, don't say no to love."

Belle remained silent for a long while, before finally saying, "I spent nearly twenty years not saying no to love, and look where that got me. There are no guarantees. I could meet someone tomorrow, fall in love, and boom, end up in the same place in five or ten years. I don't want to put myself through that again—or my kids. Let's face it, my kids will have enough up and down over the years thanks to their other mother. I don't hold out much hope for Tash's relationships."

Nikki took a sip of her drink, then said, "She was with you for the long haul. I don't think she's as commitment shy as you think."

"No," Belle confirmed. She knew Nikki was right, to a degree. "She's a serial monogamist. She was with me for so long because it worked for her. She fulfilled her sense of adventure through study, work, and travel. But when we got home, it was IVF, and then Amanda. I think she's easily bored. I just never realised it. And clearly, I bored her."

"She was only with Amanda around two years. The start date of course being up for debate. Maybe you meant more to her than you realise."

"I hope so, I really do. I hope I didn't fool myself for nineteen years. But the point is, there are no guarantees. Staying single, there's a guarantee, and I owe it to myself to have certainty. I like routine, I like predictable, I don't like my entire life being turned completely upside through no fault of my own. Well, maybe I was somewhat to blame, but you know I'd have stuck by her through thick and thin. She just didn't give me the same courtesy."

Chapter Six

THE WEEKS PASSED with Belle working on her client pro-jects, spending time playing with the children, taking them to the movies, and various play dates. One night, when the children were with Tash, Belle logged on to the computer and saw some posts in a local mums group asking for ad-vice. That gave Belle an idea, so sitting down with a glass of red wine, Belle composed a message on a Facebook group for mums she was in.

> *Hi, does anyone have advice about embryo donation? My ex and I conceived our kids through Genesis Fertility, and we aren't adding to our respective families with these embryos. I'm considering donating them—no decisions made yet—but I wondered if anyone had gone down this path? Any advice about what works best in the form of contact or not? Any disaster stories?*

Within ten minutes, Belle had finished her glass of wine and hit refresh to find a number of messages. Most were well-wishers, telling her she was providing someone with a wonderful gift if she went down this path. A couple of respondents had been recipients of donor sperm, eggs, or embryos, and reassured Belle that she was going to change someone's life forever. "So, so beautiful," one of them gushed, "it will change someone's life. I got a gift like this, and she's lying on me right now, sleeping soundly. I'm so happy, I could just burst. I thought this would never happen for me."

Belle grinned and kept reading the responses. A couple

of donors posted, and a couple of posters asked if they could PM her, which Belle responded positively to. The PMs were just people saying that they'd donated but didn't generally share their story publicly. Generally, there were no negative stories, just advice to consider carefully what type of contact Belle might want—how frequent—and try to vet the recipient to get someone on the same page. One final message said, "The trouble is that, as far as I know, you can't really enforce these arrangements. Once you sign the embryos over to them, they can make whatever decisions. It's their child. And I guess that's the way it can be, but I've heard of some people being promised the world and screwed over in the end."

Belle's heart sunk. She wanted to think of the embryo recipients as worthy people, and people she could trust. Of course, there were no guarantees in this, but Belle wondered, if some recipients were so cruel, was it really worth it? Part of her felt that her heartbreak would be far greater— not because she had no contact, but because she would have been deceived by the recipients, and the character of the people raising the baby would forever be in question. Belle chugged another glass of wine after reading that and took herself to bed. She struggled to fall asleep and had a semi-awake sleep for far too long.

She woke, feeling that she'd had insufficient sleep, but still managed to drag herself to the gym to do her cycling class before work. The following morning, Belle went to the gym again and congratulated herself on her dedication. The truth was, she wanted the mindless cycling—repetitive, and done to the beats of the music. It allowed her to switch off and forget the anxious feeling that had been nagging at her since she'd read the private message she'd received. She'd responded to every single message—even the negative one—but she'd still felt uncomfortable. She wished she could get advice from Tash, but Tash had made it clear to her that the embryos were hers to deal with. She had other people she could go to for advice, but it would be purely theoretical for them—no one, other than her and Tash, truly understood what the embryos meant, and how hard it had been for them to have a family. Tash's behaviour of late made Belle wonder if Tash even understood, or whether, in her rush to start a family with Emily, she had forgotten.

Pedalling that bicycle to the beat of 80s music, the answer became clear to Belle. It was too risky to donate the embryos. She wouldn't know the recipient and couldn't be assured of their trustworthiness. She was always saying, "There are no guarantees in life!" and this was no exception. It was too risky, and Belle was not at all a risk taker in matters of the heart. As she continued to cycle, she felt a weight lifted off her shoulders. Decision made, she could donate the embryos to science, and move on knowing she'd given it her best effort to donate.

Chapter Seven

THAT EVENING, AFTER work, Belle sat down with her pizza and glass of Coke and logged on to the computer. She frowned as she read the email in her inbox.

Hi Belle, this might come out of the blue, but I'm a member of Brisbane mums too. I know that sounds weird—you probably know I'm not a mum—but that's the reason I'm writing. For a few years, I've been trying to get pregnant. First, with my ex (Michael), and then on my own. Well,

I've thought about writing this since I saw your post on Sunday night. I've kept starting and deleting this message. Finally, I decided I have nothing to lose. I know you said you haven't decided about the embryos, but if you do decide, I wondered if you might be happy to consider donating to me. I know we don't know each other very well, but I'd be happy to be in your life as much or as little as you wanted if you were keen, and it all worked. Anyway, I'm talking too much, I know. Think it over, happy to chat, and please don't feel any pressure. I'm sure you've possibly got other people in mind, and if you don't, I'm sure you might not want someone you know. Or maybe you want someone you know better than you know me, or maybe you'd rather donate to a couple. Anyway, I better stop here. I was going to say just ignore this message if you don't want to discuss, but maybe just let me know you've received it, otherwise I'll always wonder. Just a simple "received, thanks" will be all I need to

know, and I'll leave you alone. Sorry for this out
of the blue message, and hope you're going well.
Georgia.

Belle finished reading the email, and then sat back into her chair, sighing audibly. She started to breathe deeply, baffled by what she'd just read. Belle and Georgia had met years ago—seven?—at an event hosted by Belle's sister, Alex. From memory, Alex and Georgia weren't even that close, but Belle and Georgia had clicked and added one another on Facebook that evening and occasionally 'liked' each other's statuses, but that was pretty much the extent of their friendship. Every so often, they'd seen each other at an event of Alex's, or the local shopping centre, and always chatted easily. Georgia often liked the photos of the children that Belle shared, but now she was asking to become the parent to the children's biological sibling. Belle had no idea how to feel—she'd already decided that embryo donation wasn't for her, but that was because she couldn't trust the recipient. Would donating to someone she knew change her level of trust? Could she actually bring herself to donate her embryos to someone she knew, even though they weren't close friends? She guessed she could trust her more than a stranger off the street, but what if she ran into Georgia and her child or children at the shops, or at a function, just like she had run into Georgia over the years? Would that be a good thing, or an awful thing? Belle couldn't tell. This was something she'd have to talk over with Nikki, and maybe with Alex, too, although Belle hadn't even told Alex she was thinking of donating the embryos.

Sensing the anxiety in Georgia's message, Belle wrote an email back to her the next day:

> *Hey Georgia, lovely to hear from you, and sorry to hear of your struggles. I just wanted to let you know I've received your message and am considering. I'm not even sure what I will do, but that's not about you, it's just I'm only at the research stage, so trying to decide if embryo donation is right for me. If it is, I'll definitely let you know, and I'll let you know even if I decide it's not. I hope to get back to you within the next*

two weeks. I hope you're going well, otherwise.
I'm having a lazy day here, which is lovely. Belle.

Over the next week, Belle pondered what the best plan was. She pictured a baby born to Georgia—a little girl, just like her biological sisters, or a little boy. She talked to Nikki, and finally she caught up with her sister, Alex. Alex was both surprised, but also excited. Although Alex was child-free by choice, she was an Aunty Superstar and loved babies. "Ooh, another little niece or nephew," Alex said. "That's so cool."

"But that's the thing." Belle brought Alex back down to Earth. "It wouldn't be your niece or nephew. It would be Georgia's baby."

"True. Maybe you should have a third child," Alex suggested flippantly.

"I don't really want to be a single mum to three children. Maybe you should have a baby."

"No way. I'm happy, thank you very much."

"Then, keep your opinion about my procreation to yourself. I'm not having another baby. I have no interest in having a third child." As she spoke to Alex, Belle realised that she had definitely now moved on from the idea. Now she was definitely content with her two children, which seemed like a good place to be in if she was going to donate her embryos.

"What would Mum and Dad say?" Alex asked. "Do you think it would upset them?"

"Why would it? They're my embryos."

"Oh, because it's their grandkid."

Belle shrugged at that. "They can have feelings about it, but the embryos are mine to do what I want with," she said.

"You're a braver woman than me," Alex said. "I hate upsetting them."

"Oh, no one likes to upset their parents, but I've spent my life pleasing everyone else, including Tash. Finally, I've been given complete control to decide what to do with these embryos, and I'm not going to let Mum and Dad's opinion influence my decision. It's hard enough to decide what to do." Belle and Alex's parents were actually lovely, albeit a little old-fashioned. They had coped remarkably well with

Belle's coming out and everything that came with her teen relationship with an older girl at a Catholic school. They'd coped with the two of them moving overseas, and although they'd had initial reservations about children being raised without a father, they'd been very excited when Belle and Tash had announced they were expecting. Once the children were born, they fully embraced both mums as the children's mothers, and they'd since supported Belle 100 per cent as a single mum. On the other hand, they did care a little too much about what other people thought of them and worried a little about people's 'perceptions' of their daughters, something that Belle cared little about.

"Put it this way," Belle said to her sister. "If Mum and Dad were disappointed that you weren't having kids, would you have them just to make them happy?"

"Absolutely not."

"Well, think of this as the same, but different. I need to live my life."

Alex pondered this. "Okay, I get it. So, will you do it?"

"Well, tell me about Georgia and your friendship with her. What's she really like?"

Alex confessed that she didn't know Georgia much more than Belle did. They'd met at a conference. "She teaches early years, from memory," Alex said. "Primary, anyway." Alex was a high school English, drama, and society teacher, and hoped to become a principal in the next few years, so was doing leadership courses all the time. "I met her at some resilience in education thing, I can't actually remember. It would have to have been about ten years ago. But you know Georgia, she's easy to click with. She's friendly. And so we hung out a few times, and that was when Facebook was huge, and so I added her on that. I suppose not much different from when you met her. But I've invited her to a few things, and she's invited me to some of her big events—she has a nice family. I've seen her at a few education things over the years. I thought she was like me in the kids' stakes, not a mum by choice. I suppose I assume everyone without kids is happy like me, though." Alex frowned. "She was married. Michael? Mark? Mick? I can't remember."

"Michael," Belle confirmed, remembering more from the email than anything else.

"Yeah. He seemed nice too. I met him. I was surprised that they broke up. I wonder if it was the infertility now."

Realising she was probably sharing something confidential, Belle panicked for a moment. "Please don't say anything to Georgia or anyone about this. Don't say that you know she's wanting a baby."

Alex slapped her sister's hand softly. "As if I would. Gosh, I'm not that insensitive."

Belle asked Alex whether she should do this. Alex thought for a moment and then said, "I can't tell you what to do, and I don't know what's it like to desperately want a kid, but I guess, if you have embryos you don't need, and there's someone who would love to become a mum, well, I guess it would be a really nice gift."

Belle agreed, and Alex continued. "It seems to be win-win. You make the embryo decision, Georgia gets to be a mum, and that baby gets to be born."

"But what if Georgia gets pregnant and I can't stand it? What if I'm jealous? Or…what if she has the baby and I'm heartbroken?"

Alex sighed. She didn't have the answer ready for Belle

immediately, but slowly she began to speak. "Well... I guess... I guess it's like any matters of the heart. There are no guarantees. There's risk. There's a chance you'll get hurt...but what's the alternative? You don't take a risk?"

Belle sat in silence as she absorbed this.

"I'm not really a risk taker," she finally said. "I don't even date because I don't want to endure a Tash situation again."

"Hey, I'm not giving anyone advice on romance," Alex said, laughing. Her dating history wasn't anything to write home about. "All I'm saying is, you can protect yourself for the rest of your days, or you can plunge in. Take the risk. It might be the greatest gift you can ever give someone."

Belle felt tears spring to her eyes. "True. And I don't actually want another child, so I have to remember it's a choice between giving someone something they want or... not."

Alex nodded.

"So, I guess I'll go home and tell Georgia."

Alex screwed up her face and raised her hand in protest. "Not so fast. You've bought yourself some time, you said. Give it a bit longer. Live for a week with the acknowledgement that you're giving Georgia the embryos. See how you feel over the next week. Does it sit right with you? Think about it constantly. Imagine her pregnant. Imagine seeing the Facebook post that she's had the baby. Imagine running into her and her mum, or her and a new boyfriend at the shops, happy with her baby, or angry with her toddler having a tantrum. How will you feel? Really give it that thought before you cement the decision."

Belle looked at her younger sister. "That's really great advice—thank you."

"No worries." Alex gave her sister a quick wink. "Not so silly after all, am I?"

"Absolutely not, Alexandra," Belle said in her posh voice she put on when using her sister's proper name that no one ever used, other than their parents.

"Thank you, Annabelle," Alex responded in turn, and the two sisters laughed.

Chapter Eight

ALL THE NEXT day—at work, playing with the children, showering, hopping into bed—Belle took Alex's advice and pondered how it would feel if she donated the embryo. The text message from Georgia—*I'm pregnant!*—the birth announcement, seeing them out and about. All these moments just felt right. She felt like she had an opportunity to really make a difference in Georgia's life. The only piece of Alex's advice she didn't take was to wait a week. Within two days of pondering, Belle wrote an email to Georgia.

Hey Georgia, hope you're going well. I've thought about it and am happy to donate to you. Perhaps we should catch up for a coffee? B.

Georgia's response came very quickly.

Oh, wow, you are so kind! You don't know how this could change my life (here's hoping!). Tell me where and when you'd like to meet, and I'll move heaven and earth to get there. You're truly incredible.

A few more messages back and forth, and Belle and Georgia arranged to meet on Saturday morning at the local coffee shop.

I'm going to do it, Belle texted Alex.

Great. Fantastic. Also, maybe chat to Mum and Dad before you chat to Georgia, just to be certain, Alex responded.

Too late.

Belle's response resulted in an immediate phone call

from Alex demanding to be filled in on all the details.

*

ON THE SATURDAY morning, Belle breezed into the café wearing a long green skirt and black top tied just above the waist band of the skirt. Georgia was sitting at a small table at the back of the café, clearly nervous. She was obviously distracting herself by reading a book, but it didn't look like she was concentrating very hard at all, anxiously looking at her watch. Belle was early, but she could tell that Georgia must have arrived much earlier than their planned 10:00 a.m. meeting time to have both grabbed the table at the back of the café and to be so anxiously looking between her watch, the door, and her book. Belle felt a pang of compassion for her and rushed to the table in an attempt to calm her down. "Hey." She smiled down at Georgia.

Georgia gestured to the seat. "Please, sit down. Thank you so much for meeting me. I love your outfit. You always look so amazing."

"Oh, thank you." Belle felt herself blush so rushed to explain. "Working in fashion, I always get to see new looks and how people piece together outfits. I must admit, though, I feel more comfortable in jeans and sneakers than always dressing up. I usually keep my fancier outfits for work."

"I'm the opposite," Georgia said. "There's nothing about grade one kids that makes me want to dress up. I'd just ruin my outfits, with all their paint, crayons, and stuff. I'm also often sitting on the floor, reading a book. So, I'm more likely to wear jeans to work and dress up on weekends." She looked down at her black pants and red T-shirt. "Not that I do a great job of it." She looked self-conscious all of a sudden. "Maybe one day you can take me shopping."

"Ooh, maternity wear could be fun," Belle said. "I could take you to all my favourite maternity shops."

Georgia looked a bit bashful. "I hope one day, maybe. But even if you do donate, it may not happen for me."

Belle was pensive. She was getting a little too excited for Georgia, and that probably wasn't fair, given everything the woman had been through. "Okay, I'm donating, so let's get that out of the way. You have my word. What did the doctor say, though?"

"The fertility specialist said my only chance is donor embryos. But that's no guarantee of a pregnancy, nor of a live birth. If you donate your embryos, I need you to understand that."

"Okay, let's order, then chat?"

"Oh, of course," Georgia said, and asked Belle what she wanted. Georgia insisted she would pay and went up to place the order. The two of them talked about the whole process of donor embryos, and Georgia was very upfront about her chances.

It didn't scare Belle off, though—in fact, it only made her more determined to try to help. "In some ways, I feel like I understand. It took us quite some time to get pregnant with our first, although that's nothing compared to what you have been through over the years."

Georgia told Belle she'd reached a point in her infertility that she didn't want sympathy, just understanding, and while it was difficult for anyone to understand, she liked that Belle had some understanding about how soul destroying the process could be. "It's so hard fronting up to work each day and working with kids that would be about the age my child would be if I'd been successful when we first started," Georgia said with tears in her eyes. "I love working with children. I really do, and I would never want to not work with kids, so as hard as it can be, I still love it."

Belle and Georgia talked about their relationship breakups, which had occurred around the same time—hers with Tash and Georgia's with Michael. "I think I was too focused on the infertility, and Michael lost his wife in the process. I was heartbroken, but mostly I was scared it meant I'd never become a mum," Georgia said. "So that's why I used donor sperm. I never thought I'd be a single mum, but I can't not have a child just because I'm single. It's not what I wanted, but I really want to have a child."

"I never thought I'd be a single mum either," Belle said gently. "It totally floored me when it happened and took me a long time to come to terms with it, and make it work for me. At least you'll be going into it knowing."

Chapter Nine

BELLE AND GEORGIA agreed that Belle would contact the clinic to find out the process. Then, depending on the clinic's recommendation, they would either make an appointment for the two of them, or Georgia would make an appointment to ensure everything aligned. Afterward, the embryo would be transferred, and they hoped the rest would be simple. The phone call changed things, however.

"I'm wanting to donate my embryos, and just wanted to check the process," Belle confidently said on the phone. The receptionist asked Belle for her full name. "Annabelle

Andrews," Belle said, and then heard the receptionist type into the computer. There was a long pause, and some 'thinking' sounds before the receptionist returned to the call. "Um, I'll get our senior nurse, Stella, to contact you and discuss it all with you."

Belle smiled, she remembered Stella—her favourite nurse during the IVF, a charming Irish woman. "Excellent," Belle said.

It wasn't until a few hours later that Stella phoned and told Belle that because the embryos were created with donor sperm, Belle couldn't donate them. It was Australian legislation, apparently, but it seemed like the first time Belle had heard about it.

"But I asked at the time," Belle said. "I asked because we wondered if Natasha could carry them." Tash was shocked she'd asked—she'd never intended to carry a child and was surprised that Belle thought it might be an option. But Belle wanted all bases covered, so she'd asked the question, in case Tash wanted to down the track. Now, though, Belle was completely shocked by Stella's response. She fought the tears away as she talked. To have gotten so far, and then to have the dream shattered was heartbreaking.

Stella interrupted her thoughts. "Oh, your partner? That's different. She's your partner, so you're deemed a family unit. You can absolutely donate to your partner. You just have to sign them over to her for the duration of the transfer and ultimately the pregnancy. You don't have 'rights' until you're on the birth certificate, so it's a bit strange in some ways, because they're biologically yours."

"What about a friend, or family member?" Belle asked, but Stella said that wasn't possible. Belle nearly argued back but decided not to bother. Instead, she got off the phone and sat in silence, wondering what she could do. It seemed like such a waste of the embryos to her, to just discard them. Belle got busy cooking dinner and pondering the issue. She didn't know how to break the news to Georgia, but while eating dinner, she rang Georgia, and told her that she'd tried, but it just wasn't going to be possible. "I'm so sorry," Belle said, upon hearing the disappointment in Georgia's voice.

"It's okay. I am just grateful that you offered and tried. I'll be okay." Belle could tell that Georgia was choking up and felt awful.

A few days later, the girls were going to a birthday party, next door to a big café. Belle rang Georgia and asked to meet up with her from 10:00 a.m. After dropping the girls off, Belle told the mother she'd just be next door and went to the café. "I have an hour and a half," Belle told Georgia, "and I wanted to catch up to see how you were going."

"Thank you. It was disappointing, but I'll be okay. Maybe I'll find another donor, or maybe not. I'm okay. I have a good life; I just need to come to terms with things. I've been working on it."

Belle sat silently. "It's so stupid. If we were a couple, I could do it."

Georgia started justifying the law in relation to family units and sperm donors, but Belle was only half listening. Suddenly she interrupted Georgia. "Would you do it?"

"Do what?" Georgia was confused.

"Would you pretend to be my partner?"

"Pretend to be your…your what?" Georgia asked, clearly realising what Belle meant but wanting to confirm it.

"My partner. My girlfriend. My wife." Belle grimaced,

suddenly feeling a little self-conscious. "It's probably stupid, I know that, but it might work."

Georgia just looked at Belle. She opened her mouth to speak, and then closed it again. Finally, after an awkward silence, she spoke, but all that came out were questions. "What would it mean? How? Like, would we have to tell our family and friends we were a couple or not? I'm not gay, so that would be pretty big." She looked like this was the craziest suggestion she'd ever heard, and she certainly wasn't wrong.

"No, we wouldn't need to tell our family and friends. Just the clinic, during counselling and the embryo transfer and maybe a few appointments if you got pregnant."

"And would you really want to go to that effort just to help me?"

"It's helping me too. I hate to think of the embryos being destroyed. I've thought about this for so long now, and I'm ready to donate, and they're stopping me. The beauty of things is that I'm a lesbian. The clinic knows that. I know you're not, but could you pretend to be?"

"Of course I could. My dad always said I was a good

actor." She laughed.

"We'd probably have to have counselling. Tash and I did. And they asked us questions about our relationship... You'd have to be a *great* actor."

Georgia bit her lip. "This is absurd. But I'm happy to do it."

"It is absurd. And I'd have to check that they'd let me donate to a 'new' girlfriend. Not just to Tash. I wonder if that matters."

"Would you need your ex's permission?" Georgia asked pensively.

Belle didn't think so, but it was something she hadn't considered. "Tash wanted to sign her rights away anyway. Maybe I'll ask her to do that, rather than tell her about the donation."

Georgia nodded and paused a moment before speaking. "Do you think donating would worry her? I don't want you to do anything that Tash would be uncomfortable with."

It sounded strange hearing Georgia use Natasha's nickname, given they'd never met, but Belle had really only ever

called her Tash, so it made sense that Georgia was just following Belle.

"I don't actually know. She's made it clear they're no
longer her embryos," Belle said with a shrug, "which is
weird, because they were 100 per cent ours. They may have
come from my eggs, but I held no more claim over them
than her. We did it together. And I hate making decisions
about them without her input, but she made it very clear
that she'd moved on. It seemed to be just another way of
moving on with her new girlfriend, I suppose. A line in the
sand. I'm just grateful she didn't go down this path with the
girl she cheated on me with."

"She cheated on you?" Georgia looked at Belle with
empathy and then shared a story of being cheated on before
she'd dated Michael. Belle shared how she'd felt, to have
her heart broken by the only person she'd ever dated, while
Georgia said all the right things. Georgia was really easy to
talk to, and they had a good rapport. Perhaps pretending to
be a couple wouldn't be so hard. They already had one key
ingredient of good lesbian relationships—good communication. The main thing they lacked was that Georgia wasn't

actually attracted to women, but that wasn't a problem for a fake relationship, Belle figured. Once the conversation of cheating was out of the way, the two women then started discussing their fake relationship.

"How did we meet?" Belle asked Georgia, referring to their story for the clinic and the counsellors in particular.

Georgia shrugged. "Can't we just say the truth? Through your sister?"

That would be easiest, so Belle agreed, then asked Georgia a few other questions—whether they lived together (yes), how long they'd been together (twelve months), who asked who out (Belle asked Georgia out), and they laughed at who kissed who first (Belle wanted to say Georgia). Suddenly, Georgia sat back in her seat and sighed audibly.

"What's up?" Belle asked her.

Georgia looked both sad and pensive. "I don't want to get too invested. It's all funny right now to say all of this, but anything could change. Tash might not sign them over; the clinic might say no unless it's the person you started it all with. We're making a lot of assumptions right now, but I have to keep reminding myself that it may not happen.

Hell, you could even decide you don't want to pretend-date me. Or…you could meet someone which means we can't pretend-date. This could all take some time, and our pretend relationship could last…months."

Belle shook her head. "I have sworn off relationships, possibly forever! Certainly, not until the girls are much older. I have way too much on my plate and I want them to have stability. Pretend-dating is as good as it gets for me." Belle looked away for a moment, collecting her thoughts. "To borrow your word, though, it is totally absurd. It's probably the craziest thing I've ever done."

"Too absurd? Like, it's crazy, it's time-consuming, and what's in it for you?"

"What's in it for me? I get to see the embryos have a potential chance." Belle shrugged, as if it had been a simple decision. "And hopefully you get your dream. It'll be amazing." Belle genuinely wanted Georgia to get her wish to become a mother. "As for your other worries, let me get on to the clinic on Monday, and I'll let you know as soon as I can. I can't guarantee it will happen, but there has to be a loophole if Tash is signing them across to me."

Georgia looked pensively at Belle. She then glanced at her watch.

"Good point," Belle said. "I've got to get back to the party and pick up the kids. Want to come?"

"To come?" Georgia's forehead creased in confusion. "To the party?"

"Well, to pick the kids up," Belle said, and Georgia recognised what Belle was saying.

"Oh, you want me to meet the girls?"

Belle nodded, and Georgia squinted as she thought. She briefly placed her hand over Belle's hand in a reassuring pat.

"Thank you, but no, I don't think I will. Depending on how Monday goes, I would love to meet the girls, but I think I'm better off just heading home."

Belle understood, though was disappointed to end her time with Georgia. The two bid their farewells, before Belle raced next door to find her two sugar-laden, hyperactive kids. As the children blew whistles and loudly told stories during the car trip home, Belle told herself it was probably for the best that Georgia hadn't met them in this state.

Chapter Ten

ON MONDAY MORNING, Belle dressed early and went into the office, ready to make her 9:00 a.m. phone call to the clinic. Of course, Stella wasn't available early, because the morning time was the busiest time for an IVF clinic, so Belle left a message. Distracted, she tried to focus on her work and wondered why on earth this had gotten under her skin so much. If the answer was yes or no, her life, ultimately, didn't change, and while it would be nice to help Georgia, nothing would change for her if the answer was no. Nothing, that is, other than the fact the embryos would remain unused.

After what seemed like hours, Stella finally called Belle back. As soon as Belle glanced at the phone and saw the IVF clinic's number, she made her way through the office and sat outside on a small ledge under a tree. Stella introduced herself again and told Belle she was returning her call. Belle then explained that although Tash had verbally handed the embryos over to Belle, she wanted to know what she needed to do to assure the clinic of this. Also, she told Stella, she was now in a new relationship with a new woman, and really wanted her to have the embryo transferred. Was that at all possible?

Stella assured her that it was possible, providing she had proof that Tash had indeed signed them off. Tash had to complete some forms after she had a phone call with the clinic counsellor to ensure she knew her rights and responsibilities and what she would be waiving by signing and submitting the form. It seemed fair enough, and Belle assumed Tash would be happy to do that. While still sitting outside the office, Belle rang Tash and explained what she needed, without mentioning Georgia's situation. Tash was very happy to oblige and promised she would ring the clinic immediately to arrange the phone conversation with the counsellor. By the end of the week, Tash's part of the process was complete, and though Belle had been updating Georgia via text message along the way, she rang Georgia when she was officially notified that the embryos were now completely her responsibility.

"Oh my gosh," Georgia said, and Belle could hear that she was tearing up. "I can't believe it."

Belle grinned widely. "I'm so excited!" she exclaimed. "I'm so excited for you." Belle surprised herself by realising she was choking up too.

"I have to keep reminding myself…" Georgia started, and Belle finished the sentence for her.

"That it might not happen? Georgia, just be excited for once. *This* part will happen."

"You don't understand," Georgia said. "It's been one heartbreak after another."

"I get that, but *this* is cause for celebration. You got your donor embryos. Be happy."

"I'm happy. We just need to convince them that we're

in love now," Georgia laughed. "That'll be the hard part."

"Probably a little easier for me than it will be for you," Belle said, and then mentally kicked herself for sounding so predatory. "I mean, because I'm used to dating girls. Well, a woman in particular, but I'm 100 per cent gay. It won't be hard to pretend to be into you." Everything she seemed to be saying sounded awful. "Oh God. You know what I mean…"

Georgia giggled softly. "I know what you mean. As for me, I'm a good actress, I hear—thanks, Dad. But I can't say I ever pictured me in a leading role with a woman opposite me." She laughed harder, and Belle started to laugh too. "Oh well, it'll test how convincing I am."

*

WEEKS LATER, BELLE and Georgia anxiously sat in the clinic waiting room, about to commence their counselling appointment. They also had a fertility specialist appointment lined up for Georgia immediately after counselling. Georgia would need to get scans and blood tests as well.

Belle leaned over to Georgia and whispered, "I have to

say, the fact they booked you in for the specialist immediately after counselling means the counselling isn't going to be too big a deal."

"Or they just want my two hundred and fifty bucks even if we fail," Georgia whispered back, but she was grinning.

"Annabelle Andrews," the counsellor called out to the relatively busy waiting room.

Belle and Georgia stood up. "Do we both come?" Georgia asked. The counsellor looked at them both and nodded. Belle placed her hand in the small of Georgia's back and steered her to follow the counsellor. Belle silently panicked that Georgia might have thought the physical contact was too much, but she didn't seem to react in any way. They walked toward the office door, and at this point, Belle stood back, allowing Georgia to enter the room first. Georgia smiled her gratitude at Belle.

"I'm Dr Carmichael—I'm a psychologist and counsellor," the woman said, peering over her glasses. "You can call me Penny." Penny was a new counsellor—not the same person Belle and Tash had seen all those years ago.

"Hello," Georgia said nervously. "I'm Georgia, and this is my...partner...girlfriend...Belle."

It was crazy to hear, Belle thought, after only ever being Tash's girlfriend.

Penny gave them a gentle smile. "Tell me about yourselves. That's the way I like to work here. I don't have a lot of questions, but I want to get to know you both. Then I wouldn't mind chatting to you about the implications, particularly of"—she glanced down to her papers—"embryo donation. Even though it's between a couple, we still classify it as embryo donation, and there are various implications of this I need to discuss with you both." Penny looked at the two women, peering past her glasses, and then smiled. "But that's the boring stuff. Tell me about yourselves and how you found yourself here together."

Georgia laughed nervously, so Belle spoke. "Well, my ex-girlfriend, Tash, and I created the embryos together, but she's signed them over to me. We're both in new relationships, and she's going to have a third child with her partner, and Georgia and I would like to have a third child together."

"My first," Georgia said, "but of course I'm a step-mum

to Belle's kids."

Penny looked pensive as she glanced at her paperwork. "But tell me your story. Not just the embryo stuff. Tell me about Belle and Georgia the couple. How did you get together? How long ago?"

Georgia took the lead this time. "We met through Belle's sister, Alex. Years ago, while she was still with Tash, and I was married to Michael, my ex. To be honest, I don't think either of us were interested in one another. We just met and clicked as friends. We added each other on Face book, but then we both broke up with our exes pretty much around the same time."

"Two years ago," Belle said truthfully.

"And Alex had another party—that's Belle's sister."

Penny nodded, following along.

"And I walked into that party and saw Belle. I knew she was single, and we chatted, and shared out stories—more than we'd shared on Facebook. And then, after a few drinks, we walked out on to the balcony for some fresh air. I'd never been attracted to females before, but I remember, standing out there on that balcony. She had this long white maxi dress on, her dark hair was flowing in the breeze, she had this red beaded necklace on, and I was curious."

Belle looked at Georgia, remembering that moment. The story was meant to be fiction, but this particular bit had actually happened. They'd gone out on the balcony in a group of people with wine glasses in hand. What baffled Belle the most was that Georgia recalled her exact outfit, down to the red beaded necklace. Belle gave Georgia a mixed look of confusion and surprise but couldn't speak.

"As the party quietened down, and it was just the two of us on the balcony, I placed my hand over hers"—at that moment, Georgia traced her fingers over Belle's as if to show Penny what she had apparently done on the balcony—"and we looked at one another. I suddenly hoped she would kiss me. But she didn't."

Penny sat back in her chair and sighed. "Well, that's a letdown." She laughed.

Belle kept looking at Georgia in surprise as Georgia continued.

"It was. I left that party disappointed for what might have been. I'd never been attracted to a woman before, but once I realised, I had to be with her. It took weeks to build up the courage to ask her out for a meal, and even more weeks until we had our first kiss. I soon learnt I had to make the first move." This part was clearly fictitious and had gone off the pre-planned story that Belle and Georgia had worked through—Belle was meant to have asked Georgia out, but Georgia had clearly shown Penny how interested she was in Belle, and so Belle assumed it was simply good storytelling. At least Georgia had given Belle the first kiss, which had gone along with the script—Belle had insisted it had to be that way to show the counsellor that Georgia was definitely attracted to a woman.

"Otherwise they might just think you're pining for Michael," Belle had said, to Georgia's scoffing.

"And how is dating a woman different to dating a man?" Penny asked Georgia.

Georgia nodded confidently. She was a good actor. "Yes, she's my first. And last, thankfully." Georgia glanced at Belle, smiling, and then reached for Belle's hand. "In many ways it isn't that different; in other ways, it's completely different. I feel more judged walking down the street, holding her hand. If we're not holding hands or stealing a kiss, we can 'pass' for straight, I suppose. But the main difference is that she listens more. A female partner is a better communicator."

Belle finally spoke up. "I've never dated men, but I would agree. Females talk, talk, talk."

"That's nice, though," Georgia said. "I like that we talk easily. Talk, talk, talk is nice. We really bounce off one another."

Belle was now confused about what was fact and what was fiction in Georgia's mind. Belle would certainly say they talked easily and bounced off one another well. She wondered if Georgia also felt the same.

Penny nodded. "And so you already have two children, Belle. What made you want a third?"

This question was hard for Belle to answer, particularly given she'd worked through her dream to have a third, and now no longer wanted a third child. "I didn't think I'd have a third, but then I got together with Georgia. I want her to have her dream," Belle said, "and I can give her that." At that point, Georgia reached over and squeezed Belle's hand, with tears clearly visible in her eyes. She mouthed 'thank you' at Belle but didn't speak aloud.

"And you've been wanting a child for some time?" Penny said, rustling the paperwork again and then peering over her glasses.

Georgia paused for a moment, then spoke. "It's no secret that I tried with my ex, and then a sperm donor. And then I stopped eighteen months ago, when the doctor said I needed donor embryos." Although Georgia had used a different clinic, she had told Belle she wanted to be honest about this.

"Six months later, I began dating Belle and I thought I'd just be a great step-mum. But, at one point, Belle said to me that I could use her embryos. It hadn't occurred to me. It was a lovely offer, though, and the girls get another sibling—if it works. I fully acknowledge it may not."

"How do you feel about that?" Penny asked Belle. "How would you cope if the embryo was transferred in Georgia and it didn't take, or it did and she lost the baby?"

"I'd be devastated," Belle said honestly, "but mostly for the loss of dream for Georgia. I want this baby, too, but I really want it for Georgia."

"Okay, and a nosy question. You haven't been together that long. You have a four-year-old with your ex. And, Georgia, you were married to a man not so long ago. Are you both ready for this? Why the rush?"

"Well, we're not getting any younger." Belle knew she sounded dismissive. "It's time for us. We've spent so long together; I don't think it's the length of time together, it's the quality."

"When you know, you know," Georgia said and gazed at Belle. "We know. We're meant to be together."

Penny smiled at them and continued asking them questions, and finally explained the Australian legislation against double donation. "Within a relationship, it's possible to donate, though. But, Belle, I must warn you that the embryos become the responsibility of Georgia. You're effectively signing them over to Georgia, just as Tash signed them over to you. If you broke up during IVF, which I'm sure won't happen, then Georgia makes all the calls for the embryos. But assuming you're together at the time of the birth, then you both go on the birth certificate, and are the baby's mums. I need you both to understand that."

Belle and Georgia nodded.

"But Georgia needs to make the call to add you on to the birth certificate, do you understand?"

Belle nodded again. "I understand."

"Okay, well, on that basis, if you want time to think it over, you can. If you're happy to proceed, I'll get you to sign your life away on some documents."

Belle and Georgia signed the paperwork, then made their way to the next waiting room for the fertility specialist appointment—just across the corridor. Once they'd completed some basic paperwork, they sat down in the corner of the waiting room. Belle then turned to Georgia and quietly said, "Your dad was right."

Georgia laughed. "But some of it was real."

Belle paused and tried to explain what she was feeling. "I'm just trying to work out which bits." Silence lingered in the air. What they'd exchanged in the counsellor's room had felt intimate and real, and yet, as they sat next to one another at the clinical doctor's surgery, it became apparent to Belle that she didn't really know Georgia all that well. While they had pretended they lived together and had shared a dream to grow their family together, the reality was, they'd arrived for their appointments in two cars and would go home to their empty houses separately. The reality was, Georgia was straight.

Georgia finally broke the silence. "Thank you. I feel so lucky." After the appointment was over, Georgia grabbed her car keys out of her bag. "So what's next? I get the tests, then once the results come through, we're booked in? Are you sure you want to do this?"

"Definitely." Belle was certain that she was happy to proceed, perhaps with some reservations about the pretend relationship. In some ways she felt bad about cheating the system. But she brushed those reservations away—she wasn't allowed to donate the embryos to someone unless she was in a relationship with them because of donor limits. Belle really believed donor limits could be managed whilst enabling donation to occur. She felt the restrictions were too rigid and enabled lazy donor management, rather than proper documentation. She convinced herself it was okay to cheat a system that relied on laziness, rather than proper management. Although she was generally a rule follower, she could make an exception for this.

After saying farewell, Belle hopped into her car and drove toward the office, shaking her head at the situation she'd found herself in. Georgia had been right—it would have been easier, and far less complicated, to simply donate the embryos to science. As it was, she was having to excuse herself from work meetings, and now her mind was focused on baby making again, a time in her life she'd moved on from. There's one thing about IVF that's universal regardless of the journey: it's all-consuming—it's hard to think about anything but. And, Belle reflected, even in this situation, where she wasn't personally adding to her family, her whole life had been turned upside down by the process. And yet, she wouldn't have it any other way. Deep down, she was excited about the possibility of Georgia getting pregnant. She wanted Georgia to experience motherhood, and it delighted her that her gift would help her.

At work, Belle struggled to concentrate and couldn't wait to get home that evening. She picked the children up from day care and after-school care and told them they'd get takeaway for dinner on the way home—it was easier than cooking, and the kids were thrilled.

Rather than logging in to do some more work, as she normally would after the children went to bed, Belle mindlessly watched TV, flicking the channels. She felt impatient, and yet she knew the IVF journey was slow, so she told herself to calm down, and distract herself with something fun. Remembering what she'd done just before her own IVF cycles, she decided she needed something else to focus on—a project. Just before bed, she pulled out a thick novel she'd been intending to read for some time but had been putting off. "Maybe this will do the trick," she thought to herself as she climbed into bed and turned the lamp on. She started reading the book but still found her mind wandering.

In the end, she turned the television on and just watched it, letting herself fall to sleep to some random show she had no interest in. The next morning, she chastised herself for letting television become her distraction—she could do something better than that. She was creative, and energetic. She could do a million things. Maybe she could start a podcast about lesbian matters or write a romance novel. Great ideas, but then she realised how hilarious it sounded, and laughed at both ideas. She wasn't much of a lesbian, being a single mum who never dated, and that also meant she probably wasn't the ideal romance novelist. The idea of doing anything too time-consuming was out, between work and parenting; plus, she tried to fit a few hours in at the gym each week. No, she really needed something easy to fit into her life, like baking or maybe an art project. She got ready for work thinking it over some more. Perhaps she'd just do the adult colouring in that had seemed to become all the rage. Adult colouring in front of a Netflix movie might just do the trick. Whatever it was, she just had to get her mind off IVF...and Georgia.

*

BY THE EVENING, Belle had decided on her two distraction projects—first, she was going to have a dinner in an attempt to become more social. Second, she was going to dig out her mosaic pieces and start doing some mosaic art on days when she had no plans. For now, though, she busied herself organising her first party. She wrote down menu ideas and ideas of who to invite. After a series of text messages, Belle had managed to invite seven people to her dinner party—Nikki and her boyfriend, Jason; Alex and one of Alex's close friends, Anton, whom Belle adored and Jason got along well with; Lucy, a woman she used to work with, and her wife, Kate; and finally, she invited Georgia. Although Belle was undecided about inviting Georgia, given they weren't particularly close, she thought it could be nice for Alex and Georgia to catch up; plus, she wanted to hang out with Georgia in a more casual environment. The IVF clinic wasn't exactly the most relaxed place to catch up. Thankfully, everyone agreed to come to the dinner party the following weekend, although Anton was going to be a little late due to a work function.

*

BELLE RUSHED OUT of work as early as possible on the Friday afternoon, the day before the dinner party. She headed straight to the grocery store, bought everything she needed, and then went home, and placed it on the counter, thinking about what she could make in advance and what needed to wait until the next day. She'd decided to make a few different curries, rice, naan bread, and she planned to follow it all up with sticky date pudding, not because it went with the curry, but because she loved it.

After popping music on the stereo and putting her most comfortable yoga pants on, Belle got stuck into prepping the meal. She chopped up the vegetables to make samosas the next day, and then she got stuck into making the steamed puddings ready to simply reheat the next day. With prep work complete—and dancing around her kitchen—Belle lay on the couch eating a stir-fry made of some extra veggies she'd chopped up and tofu.

On Saturday morning, she bounded out of bed, showered, and prepared for the day. She got all the prepped veggies and made four different curries for the slow cookers. For someone who lived alone 50 per cent of the time, and the remainder of the time lived with kids who would quite happily live off chicken nuggets and chips, Belle had a lot of kitchen products, and thankfully had enough slow cookers for three of the curries—a double slow cooker and a pressure cooker that also worked in slow function. She figured she could simmer the fourth on the stove, and then just keep it warm in the oven.

Hours later, the house smelt amazing, and the first guests arrived—Nikki and Jason. Nikki hated being late, if she could avoid it, so Belle wasn't at all surprised that Nikki was first. Next was Georgia. Nikki had been told a lot about Georgia, and by default, Belle assumed Jason knew a lot about Georgia, too, but when they met her, they thankfully didn't let on that they'd heard anything about her.

"Georgia is a friend of Alex's, and we've become friendly over the years too," Belle said, to ensure the conversation was kept neutral.

"Hey, Georgia," Nikki said, shaking Georgia's hand. "I went to school with Belle and Alex. Are you a teacher?"

Georgia nodded. "I teach grade one kids, and Alex teaches high school, of course, but we've met through the years at various training things. We're both suckers for those events."

"I'm Jason." Jason and Georgia also shook hands. "I'm not a teacher—I'm in telecommunications. And Nikki is in retail."

"I'm in marketing for Jaspers Pet Food. I don't even have a pet." She shook her head but was smiling. "Do you have a pet?"

Georgia's face lit up. "I have a cat, Oscar." She started flipping through her phone looking for photos, and Belle turned to face Georgia.

"I didn't know you had a cat."

"Ah, he's eight years old and the love of my life." Georgia located some photos of a fluffy grey cat.

There was so much about Georgia she didn't know — in many ways, she was a complete stranger — and Belle was grateful that she'd organised this casual dinner. A casual dinner she'd spent many hours planning, while trying to look like she'd thrown it all together. It was a nice way for her to find out more about the woman who would soon be the recipient of her donor embryos. As Nikki, Jason, and Georgia looked at the cat photos, Belle realised that Georgia must have got the cat around the time she'd also started planning for a baby. She wondered if Oscar's age was painful to think about, or whether she'd got a cat to fill the void present because of infertility.

The doorbell rang, and Georgia's phone was put away. Nikki went to answer it, and Lucy and Kate stood at the door. "Hi, Lucy. Hi, Kate," Nikki said, greeting them. Nikki had met them at various events over the years, such as the girls' birthday parties, christenings, and other family events. Lucy looked flawless, as usual, in an amazing gold-and-silver flowing kaftan, and perfect makeup showing off her bright-blue eyes, pale skin, and black hair.

Working in fashion, Lucy and Belle always ensured they wore something new whenever they saw one another. They both said that no one else ever noticed their outfits, so they had to make an effort when they were seeing one another, but that simply wasn't true. People always noticed both of their outfits when they dressed up. Lucy tended to dress up all the time, while Belle generally only dressed up when she felt like it or the occasion demanded it. She was much more comfortable in jeans. Tonight, though, she wore a flowing pink lace tunic with pink skinny-leg pants—a dressier step up from jeans, but still very comfortable.

Lucy's wife, Kate, had cropped blonde hair, lived in

jeans and sneakers, and T-shirts or hooded jumpers. Kate worked in an admin role and tended to be much quieter than Lucy, who generally filled with room, both with her dramatic outfits, but also her big, bubbly personality. Kate was generally happy to sit back and watch her wife adoringly and often with a slightly bemused expression on her face.

Alex turned up next, alone, and Belle had just got the homemade samosas out of the oven when Anton turned up. "Hey, perfect timing," Belle said. "You got here just as the food arrived."

Anton gave the group a cheeky grin. "Just the way I like it—I miss the small talk and get the food anyway."

Belle playfully punched him in the arm. He kissed her on the cheek, and they all sat in the lounge room for the starters, dipping hot samosas into various sauces. Everyone sat around getting to know one another, and Alex explained to Lucy, Kate, and Georgia that she'd met Anton on the bus back in their high school days. They'd become close friends, but nothing more, and had been by one another's side for all the highs and lows since school, from romances to careers and travel. "We went to uni at the same time, but I did teaching, of course, and Anton did small business management."

"Entrepreneurship," he corrected her, and Alex shrugged.

"And now he owns a chain of shops."

"Impressive," Georgia said, smiling.

"If by chain, you mean three very small delicatessens with grocery stores, then yes, I do."

"Wait," Georgia said. "You aren't the owner of Anton's?"

Anton nodded.

"Oh, wow. My mum and her friends go there weekly for coffee. I go sometimes with Mum too. I love it. I usually get a lemon meringue pie." Georgia grinned cheekily, her cheeks dimpling as she spoke.

As Belle cleared the plates from the starters, she watched Anton and Georgia chatting and wondered if they were flirting. Anton was a very good-looking guy, very successful, and Georgia was a beautiful woman. Both of them were very single, and very straight, but as Belle made her way to the kitchen, she couldn't help but kick herself for inviting Anton. She may as well have put him on a platter and served him to Georgia. *What an idiot.*

Belle stood in the kitchen, alone, and couldn't believe what she was thinking. She'd sworn off women and had never been interested in straight women—it was not at all her *thing*. Belle had always prided herself on the fact that she'd never fallen for a straight girl, but then again, being monogamous for nineteen years might have helped. Belle frowned as she got the dinner plates out of the cupboard. She didn't want to become another cliché.

She grabbed the naan breads out of the oven and gave herself a silent pep talk. "Do not complicate this," she told herself. "You're donating an embryo to the woman, not marrying her. She's free to date who she wants." But, Belle realised, they hadn't actually discussed how things might change for Georgia if she met someone. Belle pondered—if, for example, Anton and Georgia fell for one another tonight, would Georgia still proceed with the IVF? And what if it wasn't Anton? What if she was ten weeks pregnant and met someone? Or what if the baby was a year old? Would

Georgia still be happy that she'd got pregnant with a donor embryo conceived using donor sperm, rather than her boyfriend's sperm? Belle assumed it didn't matter to Georgia. After all, after Georgia and Michael had broken up, Georgia had commenced trying to conceive using donor sperm.

She heard Anton laughing in the next room and shook her head. She was rolling her eyes mimicking his laughter when Nikki entered the kitchen. "You okay?"

"Ugh, just Anton carrying on." She rolled her eyes to demonstrate he was annoying her, but urged herself to pull it together.

Nikki gave Belle an amused smile. "You've always loved Anton's antics."

Belle knew Nikki was right, and bit her lip for a moment. "I know; he's just grating on me tonight."

Nikki raised an eyebrow. "Would that grating have anything to do with the curvy girl with the curly hair sitting outside?"

Belle blew her cheeks out in exasperation. "Ugh, you don't mean that very *straight* curvy girl with the curly hair sitting out there? No. Gosh no," Belle said, her voice a little too high pitched, and she detected it herself as she spoke. "Now, shut up and help me get this dinner ready for people to serve up."

Within five minutes, the bench was covered with bowls housing four piping hot curries—butter chicken, a beef masala dish, a lentil dhal, and palek paneer, a spinach and cottage cheese dish. A platter of homemade naans, a large bowl of rice, and a side of cucumber raita were all there. "Everyone, come on in and dish up. We'll eat our main course at the dining table."

The dining table—usually covered in Lego, half-complete board games, or craft projects—had been cleared and perfectly set for dinner. Although it was a casual evening, Belle had worked hard to ensure that every detail was done to perfection—or as close to—while still ensuring everyone felt like they were at home. Everyone grabbed generous servings of their preferred curries and rice, many of the guests opting for a mix of all four, and they balanced the hot, homemade naan bread on the sides of their plates as they carefully carried their plate to the table. Drinks were flowing—alcoholic and non-alcoholic—and everyone was joyous.

Once everyone was served, Belle had an opportunity to grab the last seat at the table, finding herself seated next to Kate and opposite Georgia. Next to Georgia sat Anton, and beside him, Alex. "Hmm, the thorn between the roses," Belle said aloud, grinning, but not feeling particularly happy that Anton had clearly chosen to sit next to Georgia.

Anton grinned back at Belle, not noticing her attitude. "Oh, I don't know about that. I think we've got a rose garden along here." He gestured to himself as well as both Alex and Georgia.

The table of eight ate their dinner and passed on their gratitude to the chef. "If you had some free time, I'd get you to make curries for the shop," Anton declared. "They're really great."

Belle beamed. "Thank you. Unfortunately, I don't have any free time. Work is so crazily busy."

Lucy used that opportunity to segue into the fashion topic—always her preferred topic—and that resulted in small groups of people chattering away at the table, some small talk, and some more detailed conversations.

"Well, dinner was amazing," Anton finally spoke up. "Want me to wash up?"

Jason put his beer down and the table and said, "Great idea, Anton. Leave that to the boys. You girls go and relax in the lounge room. You might even get Anton making you one of Anton's Special Coffees if you're lucky."

"Ah, yes," Anton said, "good idea," and quickly grabbed coffee orders.

The women made their way into the lounge room and got comfortable. "Your house is really big," Georgia said as she glanced around the lounge room. "It's larger than I expected for a single mum of two."

"It's the house I lived in with Tash, so it was our family home. Tash wanted to be a little more footloose and fancy free, I think, so she was happy for me to keep the house. And I loved it, but it's probably a little too big for three of us, and definitely too big for just me on my kid-free week."

Georgia nodded. "Do you do tours?"

"Tours?" Belle was amused, and then said, "You want to see the house? Walk straight on through."

"No, give me a tour," Georgia said, not giving up on the idea. "Otherwise, I won't know what I'm looking at."

Belle directed Georgia through the house, while the other women chatted—all of them had seen the house before. "This is Ada's room," Belle said, showing off a bright pink decorated room. "And Cora's." Belle opened the door to a pale blue bedroom with dalmatian dog decals on the wall. "My home office," Belle said, showing off a large home office. "And the guest room here." The next room just had a large bed in the centre of the room, without a desk. "And this is my bedroom."

As they walked into the bedroom, complete with en-suite and walk-in robe, Georgia was shocked at the size of the walk-in robe. "Gosh, you could fit my bedroom in here. It's massive."

"Yes! It's what sold me on the house, to be honest. Tash gave me 75 per cent of the wardrobe when she lived here, and now I have complete ownership. I love my wardrobe."

"I don't blame you," Georgia said. "No wonder you can always dress so nicely. I have to dig for days just to find my favourite pair of black jeans." They walked back past the bedrooms to the lounge room. "Do you use your home office much? Or the guest room?"

Belle thought for a moment. "I mostly work home alone, or if the girls are in bed. I tend to work in front of the TV, sitting on the couch. Not great for my posture, but I prefer it."

"Did Tash work from home?"

"A little, but in front of the TV too. We bought a five-bedroom house in case we had three children." As soon as the words were out of her mouth, she regretted it, and Georgia had noticed. She stepped back in surprise, but the expression on her face was almost unreadable. Belle wondered if it was surprise, confusion, or disappointment, or perhaps a mix of all of these.

Belle quickly bit the bottom of her lip, and then spoke up. "We decided against a third child, obviously." The mood had shifted between them, though, and Belle didn't know what to do. How could she convince Georgia that they'd moved on from that moment, and Belle was donating the embryos with no hesitation? Surely Georgia wasn't doubting everything simply because Belle had a five-bedroom house?

Once they returned to the lounge room, Belle sat on the floor and found the women sharing funny stories about work. She sat and listened, but didn't participate, feeling awkward about the three children line. She hoped that Georgia realised that ship had well and truly sailed, and Belle was no longer keen on having a third child. That was the reason for donating the embryos in the first instance.

Thankfully, her sombre mood ended when the boys entered the lounge room with steaming coffees. They placed them on the coasters scattered around the room. "Washing up is done," Anton said. "What do you need done with dessert?"

"It's ready; I just need to serve it with the custard."

"Don't move an inch," Anton said. "It's my forte. I'll just pop in and get the desserts ready." He looked around the room as he asked, "Does everyone want one?" Everyone enthusiastically agreed, and so Anton and Jason left the room to return to the kitchen.

Belle was now relaxed, and she stretched out her legs,

leaned back, and sighed. "Mmm, I could get used to this."

Nikki laughed. "I've never seen Jason so domesticated. I need to borrow Anton to motivate him at home too." Everyone laughed in response.

As everyone tucked into their desserts, the room fell silent, except for the scraping of spoons on bowls. Not long after dessert was eaten, people farewelled and went their separate ways. Georgia held back a little, so that she was the last to leave. "I've been wanting to tell you all night — my tests came back all good. Looks like we can do this. If you're still happy, that is."

Belle smiled. "That's great, but on one condition."

"Whatever it is," Georgia said anxiously, "I'll do it."

"The condition is no more constantly checking if I've changed my mind. I did all my thinking about this before I'd ever posted that message, and certainly before I ever agreed to donate to you. The embryos are yours. And it's so great that you can proceed."

Georgia looked genuinely relieved, grateful, and happy.

*

WEEKS LATER, IT was time to commence the process, getting Georgia's cycle right with the trigger shot after weeks of medications. Three days later, Belle and Georgia sat anxiously in the waiting room at the clinic. "Reid," the lead nurse, Stella, called. Belle and Georgia stood up, and Stella glanced back down at her paperwork. "Oh, Belle, I thought I recognised you." She grinned. "And…" Stella glanced at Georgia in confusion.

"This is my girlfriend, Georgia," Belle said.

"Hello, Georgia. And your files show this is your first transfer?" The small talk continued, and soon enough, Stella said to Georgia, "Okay, so just take your pants off, jump up on the bed, and then Dr. Cooper and I will pop back, and embryologist will meet us from the freezer, and we'll be good to go." Stella swiftly left the room.

Georgia nervously glanced at Belle. "This is it, the moment that could change my life."

Belle took a deep breath. "It's strange, isn't it. One moment, it's just you and soon you could have a kid on board."

Georgia looked amazed. "I hope so. Oh my gosh, I keep

telling myself not to get my hopes up, but it's really hard. I can't help but be excited. This is probably the closest I've got. Dr. Cooper said they're good embryos."

"Yes," Belle said, nodding in agreement. She didn't add that he'd also said her infertility could be an issue.

"But let's give it a go, anyway," Dr. Cooper had said gravely, rather than optimistically. "It can't hurt."

"I just have a good feeling." Georgia beamed. "I should take my pants off."

"'That's the best offer I've had all year," Belle said jokingly, but instantly regretted it. "I'm sorry; that was creepy of me."

Georgia didn't seem to care. "I thought it was funny. Don't apologise. Truth is, I haven't taken my pants off for someone in a long time myself." Although they both laughed, the mood turned awkward, and Georgia turned a little and started to undo her jeans. Belle looked away, but once Georgia had settled on the bed with a towel over her pelvis, Belle couldn't help but admire her long, tan legs poking out of the towel. Not for the first time, Belle reminded herself to get herself together. Suddenly the door opened, and her thoughts were interrupted.

In his low, quiet voice, Dr. Cooper made some small talk with them and then told Georgia the process. "I have Stella here, and soon the embryologist will come from the freezer." The doctor gestured to another room, then opened the door and started talking to the embryologist. He then entered the room, closing the door behind hm. Stella had mentioned the embryologist coming from the freezer, too, and Belle recalled them saying it like that when they did the embryo transfers for Cora and Ada. At the time, she'd been amazed by the thought that their future babies could have been sitting in a freezer. Thinking about her girls gave her a reality hit. Soon they could have another biological sibling in the world, though not legally their sibling. The whole idea was crazy, but she still had no hesitation, just anticipation.

Dr. Cooper returned with a petite Asian woman. "This is Kathy, our embryologist." The three medical providers took their turns explaining the embryo quality, and what the process was. Stella handed Dr Cooper a blue clipboard, which he read off. "Annabelle Andrews," he said.

"Check," Kathy said as she looked at the vial she was holding. They both looked at the paperwork and then looked at the vial to compare the names. They placed the vial in view of Belle's eyes. "Please confirm your name is here."

Belle verified it was her name. They repeated the process with Georgia, ensuring it was Belle's name.

"And this embryo was created with donor sperm—donor BYY8256?"

Belle nodded. She remembered her donor's number—she'd probably never forget it—and though she'd never met her children's donor, she was grateful for him being part of their lives.

"And this is a partner donor embryo transfer, not an altruistic donor transfer."

"That's correct," Belle said, and then grabbed Georgia's hand as if to prove they were genuinely a couple—just in case there was any doubt. She smiled at Georgia adoringly.

The two women had to sign the paperwork, once again, to ensure Belle was happy to donate to Georgia.

Then, with all the paperwork out of the way, the embryol-ogist and doctor got the embryo into the speculum. Belle sat down beside Georgia's head and grabbed her hand again. Georgia seemed nervous, but it also seemed to be the right thing to do in the circumstance. Once everything was ready, the doctor slowly inserted the speculum into Georgia. Belle's previous experience of IVF had her on the bed. At the time she and Tash had done the embryo trans-fers, Belle had wondered what it would feel like to be the supporting partner, rather than the one being treated. Now Belle had some insight into it, though, of course, Georgia was not her partner.

"Now, your cervix is ready for the embryo, and… There, did you feel that?" Dr. Cooper spoke quickly.

Georgia shook her head anxiously, her eyes wide.

"Don't worry. You wouldn't really feel it, but we've just released your embryo into you. It's now onboard."

Georgia beamed up at Belle, who smiled softly at her. The two of them had held hands the entire time and didn't let go, despite the process being over.

"Now, we'll leave you in here. Stay lying here for fifteen minutes, and then we will pop in to check in and you can leave. Any questions?"

"What should I do today? I've taken today off work."

Stella gave Georgia a reassuring smile. "You can just relax. Or maybe the two of you could have a nice lunch. You're not bedridden, but I wouldn't run a marathon either. Give that embryo some time to implant. Fingers crossed."

"And no sex for a few days," Dr. Cooper added.

After the fertility specialist, head nurse, and embryologist left the room, Georgia let out a long sigh. "That was full on," she said. "I've done it before, of course, but I never really felt like it would happen then. And I know it might not now, but it feels different."

Belle felt it, too, and she knew what they said about women's instincts. "What do you think about lunch? To celebrate?" When she noticed Georgia wince a little, she added, "Or at least to help us take our minds off things? What if we go to lunch and don't discuss it at all?"

"That sounds perfect." Georgia grinned, clearly relieved. "I want to spend the next ten days not even thinking about pregnancy. I don't want my heart broken. Once these jeans are on, IVF is off limits as a conversation topic until the blood test."

"Okay," Belle said, "but can I call you every day to ask how you're feeling?"

"Nope, not unless you'd do that on any other day, and you wouldn't. So no, you cannot."

Belle laughed. She'd been caught out.

The fifteen minutes passed, and then they made their way to the carpark. Belle had driven Georgia, so that she could completely relax. They jumped in her car and drove to a little Italian restaurant Belle had recently discovered. "One of my colleagues took me here, and I love their lunch specials. I've only been coming about six weeks, but I already think I'm one of their best customers."

"Excellent, I love Italian food," Georgia said enthusiastically. Not long after ordering their meals, with a side of bread and a large bottle of sparkling mineral water, massive bowls of pasta arrived. "This looks great," Georgia said. "I love Italian. And Mexican. I love curry too. Your curry night was great." Belle thanked her, and Georgia added, "It wasn't just the food—it was nice to get to know your friends. I know I've known you for years, and I've seen your antics with Nikki over the years on Facebook, but I've never obviously met her, or even known you that well. It was…nice. I love how close you are."

Belle smiled. "That's why I invited you. To get to know you a little more and have you get to know everyone."

"Anton was great," Georgia said. "My mum was so excited to hear I'd met the real Anton. She's been going to Anton's for years. Gosh, meeting him made me a superstar with all her friends." Georgia blushed a little with embarrassment. "He's lovely, so down to earth."

"Mmmm, he is down to earth," Belle said, adding, "I've known him since he and Alex were still in high school, so before he was Anton of Anton's."

"Very impressive guy. Did you always know he would be such a success?"

"I don't think so, not when he was mucking around during the early uni days. He'd often come back to our place drunk and silly, and I certainly didn't think he was destined for greatness." Belle wasn't loving where the conversation was headed.

"Did he and Alex ever…?" Georgia trailed off, but the meaning was clear.

"I don't actually know. I wouldn't be surprised, but if anything ever happened between them, they're completely platonic now. I don't know. Alex and I don't really talk about romance and stuff."

"Really? If I had a sister, I would. She'd be my confidante. I thought you were quite close."

"We're close, but I just don't feel comfortable talking about girls. You don't really understand what it's like to be gay in a hetero world. I don't feel comfortable talking about my attraction to women."

"Really? Why?" Georgia asked pensively.

"I'm not really sure. Mostly I don't want them to feel awkward. Oh, once I'm in a relationship, that's different. I talked about Tash all the time, but if it's a crush… Actually, I don't get crushes, so I don't know."

"You don't get crushes?" Georgia looked at her in disbelief. "What do you mean?"

"Well, I might have had a mini-crush on a girl before I

met Tash. Then I met Tash and I had a major crush. We were best friends, and I was constantly thinking about her, but I thought she was straight. Then she told me she was gay, and I couldn't think about anything but her. Within weeks we were together. And then, well, that was the next two decades of my life, so of course I didn't get a crush on anyone else."

"Of course," Georgia said mockingly. "Plenty of married people are looking at other people. Getting crushes, you know."

"Not me. I'm a one-girl girl. And now, I'm a no-girl girl. I've sworn off relationships."

"You can't just swear off relationships," Georgia said. "Sometimes you meet someone and you just click. Sometimes someone takes you by surprise. I bet you didn't plan to have a relationship before you met Tash!"

"I didn't, but I'm also not fifteen anymore. I have a lot more to lose."

Georgia looked in her eyes. "What if you meet someone and you realise that you have a lot to gain?"

"I don't know what I'd do if someone I was interested

in was interested in me," Belle admitted. "But for now, my plan is I will not be dating."

"I just think you can't plan these things out. If it's meant to be, it will become apparent, and suddenly your plan will be out the window."

Belle placed her fork down beside her bowl. "I suppose you're right. But I don't have any plans to disrupt what's working for me right now. I don't have any plans to change things. I have to think about the girls, and I don't need instability in their life."

"Makes sense. Anyway, I thought he was lovely. It was nice to spend more time with Alex, too, and especially if we'll have a family connection. Hopefully."

"We aren't talking about that," she laughed, teasing Georgia.

"No, we're not, but I never did ask you. Does Alex know, about this?" Georgia gestured between the two of them. "Then once you answer, I'll shut up and we can change the topic."

Belle nodded hesitantly. "I told her, very early in the piece. I hope that's okay."

"Of course it is. I may not have a sister, but I think that's the sort of thing sisters share. You may not share dating stories, but I figured you'd have told her that you're donating embryos. I hope she's okay with it."

"She is. She's fine. I just haven't told Mum and Dad. But it's my business, not theirs." Georgia frowned, but didn't say anything, so Belle continued, "Now, what are your plans for the weekend?" Belle attempted to change the topic from IVF, not just because Georgia had initially requested they didn't discuss it, but because it felt a little awkward.

"Hmmm, I don't actually know. I'll not be out partying, put it that way." Georgia continued, "Um, I might go and see the James Bond movie."

"Nice. Nikki sees every movie ever released at the cinema, or at least it feels like that, so we used to go all the time. Lately she's been going to every movie with Jason, but sometimes she asks me. I guess Jason would be into Bond, which is a shame. I wanted to see it."

"Well, you could come with me. I don't have plans to see it with anyone."

"You don't?"

"I don't really have a big network of friends. Oh, I'm not lonely, I have plenty of friends at work, but not many I see outside of work. I spent a lot of time with Michael, and since we broke up, I've been so busy. I catch up with my cousin for dinners and movies every now and again, and she hosts regular family catch ups, but otherwise I mostly keep to myself."

Belle cocked her head. "That surprises me—you don't seem the introverted type. I mean, you became friends with Alex at a conference, and you became friends with me at a birthday dinner."

Georgia twirled a piece of hair around her finger. "Yes, but I could count on one hand how many times I've seen Alex since that event. I suppose we're friends, but virtual friendships are easier. I mean, I've never really thought about whether I'm an introvert or not. I am a little. I like people, but I prefer close friends. I'm very loyal to a friend. I don't know where you make friends when you're an adult, anyway. The fertility thing has also been a bit strange. You know… I've spent so much of my life preparing to become a mum, but not actually becoming a mum. Where do I fit in?

With mothers, or with single, childless people? I don't know where I am. Thankfully I'm very close to my cousins—they're who I talk to about it all. And my mum. Anyway, I'm certainly not lonely."

"That's good. When you say they know, do they know about the donor embryos? Oh gosh, we're really not doing well not talking about this." Belle was concerned she'd overstepped the line.

"Let's try again on the no talking on Saturday," Georgia said graciously. "Yeah, Jo, my cousin, knows. She's really my best friend. I suppose, by default, my Aunty Susan and Jo's sister Sarah also know, but I haven't told them. And Mum knows. Which means, by default, my Aunty Susan would definitely know even if Jo hasn't told her. And if Aunty Susan knows, then Sarah would know, even if Jo didn't tell her." Georgia shrugged. "Nothing much is confidential in my family, but I haven't told them who you are or anything. I just said a friend—I figure that's up to you. If it even happens, that is."

"Okay, well we can discuss that when it's a safe topic of conversation," Belle said. "So, movies on Saturday?"

Belle pulled out her phone and went through movie sessions with Georgia. They settled on an afternoon session. "So…on Saturday, am I allowed to ask you how you're feeling?"

"You would ask a friend when you caught up with them how they are, so yes, I think that's entirely appropriate. But other than that, the topic is off limits."

"Just as it was today," Belle teased, and Georgia grinned. Georgia really did have a gorgeous smile, Belle thought.

"Let me pay the bill," Georgia said, standing up to walk to the counter. "After all, you drove us here, and, well…everything else."

Belle tried to argue but quickly realised it wasn't worth it, so she gave in faster than she might normally. Belle then dropped Georgia home and went home to relax before picking the girls up from school, but she couldn't think about anything but IVF, and Georgia, all afternoon.

Chapter Eleven

BELLE STOOD WAITING at the entrance to the cinema, glancing at her phone every few minutes.

"Hi," Georgia said as she arrived. "Looking forward to this one."

"It's got some great reviews. How are you feeling?"

The question hung in the air. "I'm doing well, I had some twinges last night, my boobs are sore, and I have a good feeling." Georgia looked happy and hopeful.

"Excellent," Belle said optimistically.

The movie was action packed and held their interest the

whole time. Afterwards, they had lunch together, and, not for the first time, Belle thought Georgia was quickly becoming one of her closest friends. Belle wanted to spend as much time as possible with Georgia, and yet, she was aware that she was donating embryos to Georgia and wanted to maintain as much distance between them as necessary for Georgia to have the dream of parenting she always wanted.

Georgia had a heap of questions for Belle about being a single mum, but they weren't easy for Belle to answer. As she told Georgia, she'd never set out to be a single mum, so they had one major difference there. "At first, I was a little excited about having *me* time when we broke up. I'd given so much of myself to our relationship, and then our girls, I'd lost a big part of myself. Like I've just started doing mosaic again for the first time since I was a teenager. I probably wouldn't do that if I was still with Tash. I think I lost myself a little in that relationship."

"So you like the fifty-fifty?" Georgia asked, frowning. She was possibly worried about how she'd juggle it all on her own.

Belle shook her head. "I hate it. Absolutely hate it. I

didn't set out to be a fifty-fifty parent. I didn't set out to miss half of their life. This was not what I wanted for them, or me. I wanted the old-fashioned dream—well, other than the two mothers part," she laughed. "But as old-fashioned as you get otherwise. And here we are. It works. The girls have adapted to it, and possibly remember no different. The break is nice. Time to focus on work, and a bit of downtime." She shrugged. "But to miss the morning of their birthdays, or sharing Mother's Day across two houses? It's so hard." Georgia looked at Belle sympathetically, and Belle looked away so she didn't start to cry. "When Tash and I were together, every decision about the girls was made together—down to what they'd eat, what time they went to bed, what to give them for birthdays, or what clothes to buy them. We were both so involved. And now I miss so much, and so does Tash, but I'm happy they have two really engaged parents. Don't get me wrong. Tash and I co-parent together well, which I'm so grateful for. We communicate a lot, and we get along well. I sometimes think she makes crazy decisions—mostly around the women in her life and the speed at which she seemingly rushes in, and subsequently rushes out." Belle wrinkled her nose. "But she's a good mum. We're lucky."

Georgia looked thoughtful. "It would be hard, though. Suddenly your dream changed. Of raising kids with your wife, and bam..."

"Partner, not wife. We never did marry, but we were as good as. But yes. That's exactly right." Belle smiled sadly. "It's a common reality. Many families are doing it. My girls aren't the odd ones out at school, or anything. But it's not the life I imagined when I pictured having kids." Georgia really seemed to get it and was happy to talk about it. "I'm sure you have dreams about parenting—if it all works out, what type of parent you'd want to be."

"In the early days I think I did. But now, I'm just so focused on cycles and fertility meds, and so on. I haven't dared to think beyond the immediate goal."

Belle raised her eyebrows. "Impressive."

"Not impressive." Georgia twirled her hair around her finger as she continued. "I'm just doing the same as you. I'm just protecting myself from heartbreak. It's just mine isn't related to romance."

Chapter Twelve

BELLE HAD HAD half a day of back-to-back meetings and was finally eating a ham and salad sandwich at her desk while flicking through emails. The big fashion week event that Belle coordinated was coming up in eight weeks, and she was putting finishing touches on flyers, press releases, and other promotional materials, so she'd received a series of emails requesting urgent proofing. As she bit her sandwich, she tried to respond one-handed. Her mobile phone beeped with a message beside her, and the screen flashed up with Georgia's name. Belle placed her sandwich down on her lunchbox and lifted the phone to read the message.

No luck this month ☹ the message said.

Belle's eyes widened, and she realised that Georgia had had her blood test. She wasn't pregnant. As the news sunk in, Belle felt awful for her friend. She picked up the phone and rang Georgia immediately, but after a series of rings, the call went to voicemail.

Belle responded by text. Where are you?

At work. But I'm heading home soon. I can't focus on teaching this afternoon, Georgia responded.

Belle quickly proofed the urgent emails, packed up her stuff, and finally wrote back to Georgia.

Can I pop in?

No need, I'm not much company, but come if you want.

*

TWENTY MINUTES LATER, Belle rushed into a supermarket and grabbed a bright bunch of flowers and a gossipy magazine off the shelf. She then rushed back to her car and drove to Georgia's house. She knocked on the door.

"Come in," came the muffled voice from inside. "It's unlocked."

Belle walked into the lounge room. The curtains were open, but the lights weren't on, and the house seemed dark. Belle had only ever been outside the house, so she wasn't sure if the lounge room was usually this dark or not. Perhaps it was Georgia's mood that made Belle feel that way. The whole room felt sombre.

"Hey," Belle said. She tentatively sat down beside Georgia and then placed the flowers and magazine on the coffee table. "I brought you some…stuff to hopefully cheer you up a little…" Suddenly the ideas that flowers or celebrity news might lift the mood of someone who had just had awful news seemed ludicrous. It was a token gesture at best but seemed almost insulting once she saw how defeated Georgia looked.

"This is awful," Georgia said and released a sob. She shook her head, as if the whole thing was crazy. "I shouldn't have got my hopes up, but somehow, I thought that being your embryos—your embryos that had created so much life in Cora and Ada—would allow me to have my dream. Somehow, I thought that not coming from my useless eggs, everything would be okay." She sobbed again. "How... wrong...I...was!" Georgia spluttered. "How...wrong...I... was! My body...my body... It betrayed me...not the embryos." Now she was crying so loudly, and Belle couldn't make sense of any further words, so she just patted Georgia on the back.

It was painful to see her friend so upset. In some ways she felt responsible. They were her embryos that had given Georgia the hope, after all. Logically she knew that wasn't the issue, but her heart ached for her. She put her arms around Georgia, and Georgia fell into them. Belle shut her eyes, allowing herself to melt into the embrace. They stayed like that for about fifteen minutes, and finally Belle got up and went to the kitchen. She pulled together a basic dinner for Georgia to heat up later, covered it in cling wrap, and put it in the fridge. She then did a quick tidy of the kitchen and went back to the lounge room. Georgia hadn't moved. Belle asked Georgia where she kept her vases, and arranged the flowers into a vase, placing them on to the coffee table in the centre of the lounge room.

"Want me to stay?" Belle asked.

"You've probably got to pick up the girls."

"Tash has them this week."

"Oh, well, I'm sure you have better things to do. I'm not much company."

"We don't even have to talk," Belle said. "I'm not expecting amazing entertainment. I'm just concerned for you. We could watch a TV show." Belle reached for the remote.

"Maybe I'll have a soak in the bath," Georgia said. "Read the magazine you bought. If that's okay?"

Belle frowned. "You sure you'll be okay? You won't fall asleep in there or anything?"

Georgia assured her she'd be okay, so Belle told her about the plate of food and went to run her a bath. Once the bath was ready, Belle got up to leave. "Please call me any time of the day or night, even if you just want to cry while I sit on the other end." Belle walked forward and hugged her. It was amazing how natural it felt to embrace her.

As she drove home, singing to the music in her car,

Belle couldn't help but think how sad she was for Georgia. She had really wanted this to be Georgia's happy ending. Belle had desperately hoped that she could have given Georgia that. She had failed her friend.

*

HOURS LATER, AFTER logging in to do some work at home, Belle got her own dinner ready. While she cooked, she rang Nikki. "Georgia didn't get pregnant."

"She didn't?" Nikki sounded disappointed. "What's the plan now?"

"I didn't want to talk about the next cycle with her just now, but I'm hoping that she'll jump straight in again. I know that helped me, but Georgia's situation is different. She seemed really affected. Really resigned that it was over, so I'm a bit worried."

"She needs to give it three goes, I think," Nikki said, plucking the number out of thin air.

Belle had slightly more understanding of the heart-break of infertility than Nikki, so wasn't sure Georgia would be up to that. When Tash had asked Belle to give it six goes, Belle hadn't believed she had it in her. But Georgia had been doing this a lot longer than Belle and had experienced so much more heartache than Belle ever had. "Maybe," Belle said. "I'm sad for her, but still hopeful. The embryos are good. I hope Dr. Cooper has a plan for the way forward."

*

DR. COOPER DID recommend a new medication for Georgia. "Also," he said, in their next appointment, "your progesterone was quite low this cycle. We increased your progesterone during the cycle, but it didn't work. Let's change the drugs next time."

"Is it hopeless?" Georgia said in a very small voice. Belle looked sympathetically at her and reached over to squeeze her hand.

Dr. Cooper shook his head. "I'm not in the business of giving my patients false hope, but I've seen some women really succeed with donor embryos."

"If it was going to succeed, wouldn't it have happened this time?" Georgia asked. She wanted permission to give up. Once again, Dr. Cooper shook his head.

"Even with all the right conditions, every attempt doesn't result in a baby. You have about a 40 per cent chance of success at your age, but that's a 60 per cent chance of failure. Plus, we're dealing with infertility, donor embryos, and low progesterone here. We can improve the low progesterone and make sure your body is fully prepared. I see no reason not to go again next cycle."

"Next cycle?" Georgia hadn't expected this.

Dr. Cooper smiled. "All we need you to do is ring us on day one, and we'll start the process again." He winked at her. "Keep resting, stay as stress free as you can, eat well, exercise, but not too much, and leave the rest to us. And you"—he turned his attention to Belle—"take care of your girlfriend. Cook her meals, give her foot rubs, pamper her. Whatever she needs."

Belle smiled and patted Georgia's hand. "You got it."

After they left the surgery, Belle asked Georgia what she would do. "I guess I just follow doctor's orders." She shrugged. Belle kept holding Georgia's hand as they walked down to their cars. She was surprised it didn't feel awkward at all. In fact, it felt nice.

Chapter Thirteen

"YOU WORE A skirt today."

"Less awkward than trying to get out of jeans in front of you." Georgia laughed. "All I need to do is pull my knickers off, and this"—she swirled her long skirt around her legs—"gives me all the privacy I need."

"Away from the eyes of the perverts."

"Hey, you said it, not me."

Belle was pleasantly surprised that Georgia was in a joyful mood. She had cracked a number of jokes in the waiting room. Belle had half expected the mood to be sombre between them as embryo number two was transferred, but Georgia was very relaxed.

"How are you feeling?" Belle asked.

Georgia screwed up her mouth, thinking before she spoke. "I don't know. Resigned, maybe. What will be will be. Mum reminded me I have a happy life, that if it doesn't happen, it doesn't happen. I'll always wonder, but I think we'll give it three goes, then give up?" She said it as if it were a question awaiting Belle's approval.

"Your decision," Belle said. "Your embryos." She smiled.

Stella called them into the room and cracked a few jokes with them. "Dr. Cooper will be here soon, and the embryologist, so you know the drill. Get yourself comfortable, and up on the bed." As she left the room, Georgia swiftly reached up and removed her knickers, put them in her handbag, and zipped it up. She was clearly feeling proud of her foresight. She jumped up on the chair, pulled her skirt up around her hips, placed the modesty towel over her, and spread her legs, ready for the doctor. It looked to Belle that Georgia was becoming much more relaxed about the process.

"It's crazy—they give you a modesty towel, then ask you to be spread-eagled as they reach up as high as they can into you," Georgia said, laughing. Belle blushed, though she was certain she'd cracked the same joke to Tash when she had been sitting on the IVF bed herself.

Dr. Cooper and the embryologist, this time a tall red-headed lady named Tara, entered the room from the freezer. They reported on the status of the embryo and confirmed the identity of both Belle and Georgia before requiring sign off. Then, the speculum was entered into Georgia.

"And it's released," the doctor said. "Now all we want you to do is relax in here for fifteen minutes, and then you're free to go. And remember, avoid hanky-panky for the next few days." He looked at Belle, who nodded in response. Pleased that everything was under control, Dr. Cooper, Tara, and Stella then left the room, leaving Georgia lying back in the chair while Belle kept holding her hand.

After wasting time chatting about anything and nothing, Belle finally looked closely at Georgia.

"You okay?" Belle asked pensively.

Georgia's mouth turned upwards. "I don't think I've heard someone say 'hanky-panky' since I was a teenager and started dating. My dad used to say it." She cracked up laughing.

"Were you a bit of a naughty girl?" Belle asked, teasing Georgia.

"Hmm, I gave my dad his fair share of grief, that's for sure. I dated a lot, my poor dad."

Belle laughed. "I bet you did. I was such a good girl."

"A good girl that was shagging the girls at her sleepovers."

"Oh God." Belle smirked and then clarified, "One girl. I'm a one-girl girl, I've told you that." They grew silent but looked at one another. The tension between them was evident to Belle, at least. She wondered whether Georgia had realised how important she had become to her. She wondered if Georgia had noticed her growing affection for her. She wondered what Georgia thought about her.

Breaking the mood was a tap at the door, and Stella hollered, "That's your fifteen minutes; you're free to go." She handed Georgia the progesterone, and they made their way to the car.

"And another one down," Georgia said. "I know I said I wasn't going to analyse anything last cycle, but I did. This time, I'm pretending it didn't even happen."

"Good idea," Belle agreed. "But do we still go for a celebratory lunch?"

"No," Georgia said, and Belle was disappointed. "We just go for lunch."

"Ah! You got me. I thought you were saying no to lunch."

"Not at all. But today, no classy Italian place. I want to go to the greasiest burger place we can find."

"Excellent. Did you have somewhere in mind?"

Georgia shook her head.

"Good, because I've got just the place."

The two of them jumped into Belle's car and made their way to a little hole-in-the-wall burger bar with a few tables and chairs scattered outside. Once they were seated, they barely drew breath until the big platters of burgers and chips were placed in front of them. Then, silence.

"This is amazing," Georgia said about her beef and

bacon cheeseburger when she finally spoke. Belle nodded in agreement but didn't speak, enjoying her Mexican beef burger too much. At some point, they each cut off a portion of their burgers to give one another a taste and determined that the beef and bacon cheeseburger was the winner.

After the bill was paid, by Belle this time, she said, "Well, best get you home in front of the TV."

Georgia didn't argue. She told Belle that the idea of crashing out on the lounge sounded blissful. "Work has been so busy. I suppose it has been for you too."

Belle rolled her eyes. "Crazy with the fashion gala. I've been living and breathing it. Are you still coming?"

"Yes, I'm really looking forward to it." Belle had invited Georgia to the annual fashion gala which was on the following Saturday night. She figured it would take her mind of the IVF and give her an opportunity to spend some time with all the people she'd invited to the dinner party. It was always a fun night, a big night to look forward to in the fashion world. Belle really couldn't wait.

Chapter Fourteen

AFTER PICKING UP the children on Friday evening, Belle made pizza dough, and the three of them made homemade pizzas while dancing to music on the home pod. Ada wanted just cheese on her pizza, Cora wanted bacon and cheese, and Belle piled hers high with vegetables and bacon. Once they were baking in the oven, she picked her phone up and noticed a message from Tash.

Hey, what are you girls up to tomorrow?

No idea. Belle responded. *Nothing much. I thought we*

might just potter around the house. Why, what's up?

It wasn't unusual for Tash or Belle to check in, especially after handover, but the way Tash specifically asked about plans for Saturday made Belle wonder what Tash wanted. She didn't have to wait long, as Tash responded quickly.

I was hoping to pop in and have coffee, catch up, see the girls.

Again, this wasn't out of the ordinary, so Belle readily agreed. She also wondered if Tash might want to come to the gala—she always had before, even once Belle and Tash had broken up—so decided she would ask her the next day.

*

A KNOCK AT the door interrupted the most elaborate train track set-up Belle had ever coordinated. They had a mini-village, with shops and a park. "Wow, this is impressive. You must have been up for hours," Tash joked.

Belle yawned. "Don't laugh. Someone got up super early today." She gestured at Ada. "She climbed into my bed, and I couldn't get back to sleep. Eventually we had breakfast and started this village. Cora, thankfully, didn't join us until about eight."

After hugs with each of the girls, Tash suggested they go into the kitchen for coffee. "Sounds good," Belle said, and after more cuddles, the girls were happy to keep playing with the stereo on in the background. Belle put the coffee machine on—the pod one that Tash liked. Tash went straight to the pantry to get the biscuit barrel out. Although they'd broken up, Belle liked that Tash still felt comfortable in their old family home, and that there was really no formality between them. It helped the girls to see how comfortable their two mums were around one another.

Tash sat down with her steaming coffee in her hand and the biscuit barrel between them. She pulled out a chocolate-coated biscuit. "How are you going? You must be busy?"

"I am. The gala is next Saturday night, so if you want to get a babysitter, you and Emily are welcome. Or Emily could watch the girls. But no pressure."

"Thanks, I'll chat to her and let you know by Monday."

Belle was finalising numbers, but two extras wouldn't cause an issue, especially as she knew people would drop out in the lead up to the event.

"How are you going?" Tash asked again.

Belle looked at her in confusion, surprised that Tash had asked the same question twice in about two minutes. "Good, busy, like I *just* said. How are *you* going?" Belle assumed Tash had something to say.

Tash laughed. "Sorry, I have a lot on my mind—I'm clearly forgetful. I'm good. Everything's good. Ahh... well...Emily's pregnant." Tash looked embarrassed.

Belle opened her mouth in surprise, and then kicked herself for not realising when she'd received the strange text message the night before. She stood up and gave Tash a hug. "Congratulations, Mum!" She grinned, genuinely happy for Tash, though recognising that it was all quite awkward. Until she'd got the warning from Tash, she'd never imagined her starting a new family. To Belle, whether Tash and her last girlfriend, Amanda, had more children or not was probably the least distressing part of that relationship, but it had never seemed to be on the agenda. When it came to Emily, though, children had been the plan so early in the piece. Belle only hoped that meant stability for Tash. "Is it the same donor?" Belle assumed it was, but just wanted to know for certain.

Tash grinned. "Yep! Worked first go."

Belle instantly felt sad for Georgia upon hearing this but tried to push that aside and be happy for her ex. "That's great." She knew Tash probably noticed the slight edge to her voice. "Really great."

"You okay?" Tash reached out, grabbed Belle's hand, and stroked the back of it. It was an intimate moment that reminded Belle of stroking Georgia's hand during the embryo transfer. Belle nodded, but tears sprang to her eyes. She willed them away, concerned Tash would misunderstand. She didn't want to share the story with her—it wasn't Belle's story to share. Tash looked concerned but knew Belle enough not to talk about it, so she remained silent. Instead, the matter got brushed aside, like so many things between them had over the years.

"How's Emily?" Belle asked, trying to change her focus. "She must be so excited."

"Great—she's nearly eleven weeks now, and she's started getting sick, but she's doing really well. I remember how tired you were at this point."

"Don't remind me. I practically fell asleep the moment I'd get home from work."

"Practically? You did fall asleep. I'd cook dinner and need to wake you."

Belle bit her lip as she reflected on that time. It had been such an exciting time in their lives, and she was pleased that Tash and Emily were happy enough together to go down this path, even if it did feel a little strange that Tash would be welcoming a new child without Belle by her side.

"Have you told the girls? Have you told your parents?"

"I haven't told the girls. We wanted you to know first, and if you're happy for me to, I will."

Belle nodded her consent.

"And I told Mum and Dad." Tash winced a little, which made Belle laugh.

"How did they feel?"

"Look, I think they're excited—you know they're proud grandparents. But I think they think we rushed in.

And let's be honest, we all know we did. But we're lesbians and we're not getting any younger."

Belle couldn't stop smiling at the lesbian comment — the joke about 'what do lesbians take on a second date? A moving van' was frequently so true, though not at all something Belle was interested in.

"Mum and Dad are a little concerned and worried about how the girls will cope to see me with a child full time when I only have them 50 per cent," Tash said.

Belle took a sip of her coffee. "That's a good point. Have you thought about talking to them about that?" She'd always liked Tash's parents and found they always made rational points, especially when their daughter was being a little too spontaneous. But now the horse had bolted, so to speak. Soon enough, the girls would have another sibling. Belle only hoped it would all work out well for Tash and Emily.

Tash responded, "I think it's a good point, and I'll certainly weave it into the conversation with the girls." Tash wasn't an idiot, she'd be able to handle the conversation, but Belle still worried for how the girls would handle it.

"Do me a favour?" Belle said. "If you're getting a babysitter for them next Saturday, don't tell them about the baby before you head out." Belle knew that Tash and Emily would get the children on Friday night, and so she was concerned they might make the announcement on the Saturday and then head out to the gala, leaving them home with a babysitter, or with Emily.

Tash was pensive. "That's a good point, actually. Maybe we could take them out on Wednesday afternoon or something? Straight from school, and drop them to you? Then they can have some you time to talk too. I don't know, let me talk to Emily and I'll let you know."

Belle agreed. In some ways, that could be a good way for Tash to break the news to the girls, and they could come home and have some time with just Belle, and maybe share how they were feeling. They were still so young, though; she figured they'd be excited. On Wednesday evening, Belle was pleased that she was correct—they were completely fine. They told Belle how excited they were to have a baby, and Ada said she was looking forward to being a big sister. It seemed that Tash and Emily had included them very well in the pregnancy excitement. Belle was impressed. Maybe Emily would be a good influence on Tash, or maybe she'd underestimated Tash's ability to put the girls before her own needs.

Two days later, Belle walked out of work at six, determined to have the evening off. Everything was in place for the next evening, and she was looking forward to seeing her hard work come to fruition. She checked in with her table of guests, and everyone was still attending. Tash and Emily had organised Tash's parents to have some grandparent time and babysit the girls, so they were both coming. Belle was a little anxious about this—she'd invited them before finding out that Emily was pregnant, and given they'd be at the same table as Georgia, she probably wouldn't have invited them if she'd known. Emily would be nearing the twelve-week mark now, and now that everyone in their families knew, Belle was aware they might start sharing the news more widely. She tried to not panic about that, but aside from all the plans rolling out as she'd planned, she couldn't help to be a little concerned that the night could be ruined for Georgia.

Belle sat on the couch and called Nikki, filling her in on the potential drama. "Maybe you should tell Georgia in advance," Nikki suggested. "Or you should just try to avoid them sitting together in any way. Put me between them. I'll keep the conversation flowing and stop any potential conversation between them."

Belle laughed at that idea; she could just picture Nikki jumping in and talking over the top of them, even when one of them asked the other to pass the salt or something.

"Have you told Georgia not to say anything to Tash about the embryo transfer?"

"No, I haven't, but I don't think Georgia is sharing it widely. She should know on Monday whether this cycle worked; I doubt she's running around advertising it. She doesn't even want to talk about it. And I'm not telling Tash until I know if it's happening. There's a good chance it won't happen."

"Fair enough," Nikki said. "I hope it all goes well." She sounded anxious.

"You were meant to reassure me," Belle said, laughing as she ended the call.

Chapter Fifteen

BELLE STOOD AT the entrance of the function room.

"Stop stressing. Everything is done, the room looks amazing, and you look so incredible!" her assistant, Jamie, said.

Belle's hair was pulled back in a sleek updo, and she complemented the dramatic hairdo with a plunging red dress that fell to the floor. "Thank you. I'm just anxious about numbers, about the food arriving on time, about the drama queens that might not win awards..." She didn't mention a potential pregnancy announcement too.

"So, basically you're anxious about everything." Jamie gave Belle's arm a squeeze. "Calm down. It will be an amazing night. Always is. And quick, the first of the guests are arriving now." Jamie peered past Belle, to the clear elevator that was coming up to twentieth floor. "Get your game face on now, girl," he said. "Prepare to greet your guests."

*

BELLE WAS ALREADY worn out and had only greeted about half her guests. Nikki, Jason, Lucy, and Kate had already arrived. Nikki and Jason were seated at the table of ten that Belle had organised with her friends. Lucy and Kate were seated with others from the fashion industry that Lucy knew. Soon Belle's family arrived—her parents, Clive and Julie, along with Alex. They all embraced Belle hello.

"You look incredible!" Alex exclaimed, and her parents agreed. This resulted in Belle complimenting them all— Alex was wearing a short purple floral dress which looked great against her short, blonde hair while their mum was wearing a lovely black dress with orange jacket. All of Belle's friends and family dressed up for the annual gala.

Even her dad, usually seen in tradie wear or jeans and polo shirts, was in a bow tie. Belle pointed them toward the table, and soon she noticed them greeting Nikki and Jason out of the corner of her eye. There was no time for Belle to chat, as she had more people to greet.

After Belle had been talking to her former boss for some time, Georgia stepped in front of her. She looked gorgeous in a strapless glittery silver dress that went to the knees. "Hello," Belle said, embracing her. "You look perfect. Really perfect. I've got you at Table 2, with Mum, Dad, Alex, Nikki, and Jason, who you know. Tash and her girlfriend, Emily, will be at the table too." Belle suddenly kicked herself for not briefing her parents about Emily's pregnancy. She'd been so busy thinking about Georgia that the idea of her parents finding out hadn't occurred to her. But now Belle had to greet the next set of guests, so could only hope that Tash and Emily weren't ready to announce their happy news.

*

"THIS AWARDS EVENT is the highlight of my calendar

every year," Belle spoke into the microphone once everyone was seated. "This event is why I do what I do. Seeing the worthy recipients receive their awards is one of Australia's most exciting fashion moments. And seeing what Australia's fashion elite wear each year is always inspirational. You do me proud. Tonight, we'll be partying, and we'll be celebrating our award winners, but scattered through the night will be amazing food, served in an alternate drop." Flashes kept going off as various photographers snapped photos for the fashion pages of newspapers and magazines. "Menus are on the table. For now, the drinks are flowing. Please sit back, relax, and enjoy. We'll be dancing later, so save your dancing feet for then." And with that, Belle headed toward her table for the first course.

As she approached the table, she noticed Tash was holding court, surrounded by many of the people that meant the most to Belle. Belle rolled her eyes, hopeful that Tash's out-there behaviour wasn't causing issues for anyone at the table, Georgia in particular. Thankfully, once she sat down, she realised that Tash was doing a fabulous job of trying to get the table all interacting.

"You did brilliantly up there—I'm so proud of you," Belle's mother said to her.

"Aww, thanks, Mum." Everyone chimed in, agreeing with Julie.

"It's an impressive event," Georgia said, glancing around the room.

Belle was so happy to hear that the event she worked hard on each year was impressive to her friend. "Thanks," she said, beaming back at her. The first half of the evening passed in a blur.

Jamie came up to the table and whispered to Belle, "You're up in ten minutes."

"Ten minutes," said Tash, and then she glanced at Emily.

Here it comes, Belle thought, holding her breath. She wasn't just worried about Georgia's reaction, but now her parents' too. Finding out their grandchildren would have a new sibling unexpectedly was something she should have really warned them about. Come to think of it, she probably should have warned Alex too. She let out a deep breath and braced herself.

"Well, I'm pleased you all got the opportunity to meet Emily this evening. She's become a very special part of my life," Tash said. Belle couldn't help thinking it was a bit rich using her event at the platform for her ex's baby announcement, but that's the way Tash rolled—completely self-absorbed. Tash wouldn't have meant anything bad by it—she just wouldn't have realised. "She's so special that we decided to grow our family."

Belle's mother audibly gasped and grabbed Clive's hand. Belle shot an apologetic look at her.

"We're having a baby in October." Everyone congratulated her, then glanced over to check for Belle's reaction.

After congratulating Tash and Emily, Julie turned to her daughter. "Are you okay?" she whispered.

Belle nodded. "I already knew. I should have said—I didn't think." Although Alex had joined the conversation by this point, Belle was looking past them, trying to read Georgia's reaction, but she was up talking animatedly to Tash and Emily and seemed okay. She didn't look like she was going to crash in a heap.

Belle was eager to check in with Georgia, but before she

had the opportunity, Jamie rushed to the table. "Belle, you're up."

*

BELLE ANNOUNCED THE next series of awards, posed for the obligatory photos, and then raced to the bathroom. Normally she'd have done a last-minute loo run before getting up on the stage, so she was particularly annoyed with the timing of Tash's announcement. Not only was she desperate to relieve her bladder, she was also anxious that she hadn't had time to check in with Georgia, nor complete her conversation with her mother and sister. She only hoped they were all coping okay with the news, and none of them were upset by it, Georgia in particular.

As Belle left the restroom, she made her way back toward the function room, nearly running into someone on the way back. "Georgia," she said, surprised. Georgia walked toward Belle, practically cornering her in the end of the hallway. "You okay?"

"I wanted to have a chat," she said, "away from prying eyes." The way Georgia looked at Belle threw her. She certainly didn't look unhappy; she looked happy and almost flirtatious, Belle thought. Surely Georgia wasn't going to pin her up against the wall and have her wicked way with her. The thought made Belle both full of anticipation and laugh at how crazy she was becoming. Georgia wasn't speaking; she was looking around for somewhere to sit.

"Are you really okay?" she asked again.

Georgia looked at her intently. The two sat on a bench chair back near the restroom entrance. Georgia crossed her legs and sat up tall. "I'm okay. How's your night?" she asked. Belle couldn't believe Georgia was sitting her down just to check in. "I suppose you're busy?"

Belle simply nodded in response.

"Sorry, I suppose you don't have time for a chat."

"It's the perfect time for a chat, but I only have five or ten minutes. Soon we'll be announcing the next lot of prize winners. You're worrying me—are you sure you're okay?" Belle frowned. "Is it Tash and Emily? Their news?"

"No, I'm happy for them," Georgia responded, smiling.

"Really? Okay, but I know that kind of news could

be…difficult."

"It could be, but I'm in a good mood." She smiled and looked in Belle's eyes. "Belle, I'm pregnant too!"

"Huh? But the blood test is Monday." Belle smiled widely but wasn't sure if this was some kind of practical joke. Of course, there was no way this was funny if it was a joke.

"I peed on a stick yesterday. I know, I said I wasn't going to. There was a faint line, so I rang the clinic who asked me to come in for a test today. And they said I'm pregnant. I need to have another test Monday to see how the levels are going, but for now, I'm bloody pregnant. Right now, I'm more pregnant than I've ever been."

"Oh my God," Belle said and hugged Georgia. "I'm so happy for you! Such wonderful news."

"I'm so happy, too, but also cautious," Georgia admitted.

"I have a good feeling." Belle embraced Georgia again. "Be cautiously optimistic."

"Cautiously optimistic. I like that. Now, you best run back to your work."

"I'm going to be grinning like a fool up on stage. I wasn't expecting this tonight," Belle admitted, "and I panicked when Tash told me the news. I was worried that it would be distressing for you if they revealed it tonight."

"Tash is really nice, and she's really excited about her new baby. It's nice to get to know her, actually," Georgia responded.

Although Belle didn't want to be in a relationship with Tash, it still stung a little to hear how excited Tash was to be having a third child. "She is nice. I'm pleased you like her. It's nice you get along. She was a big part of my life for so long, and you're a big part of my life now." The sentiment was nice, though the comment came across a little more seriously than Belle had intended, and she instantly panicked, but Georgia seemed grateful for the comment. Belle figured in her happy mood Georgia probably hadn't even noticed the intensity of the comment.

"Okay, back you go. We can check in again after Monday."

"Monday?" Belle said. "I'll be checking in with you tomorrow."

Belle told herself she'd be this excited for any friend that had just found out she was pregnant after trying for so long.

Chapter Sixteen

THE REST OF the night seemed like a blur of photographs, awards, music, drinks, handshaking, and a bit of dancing. Once the formalities were over, Belle hit the dance floor with her sister and mother but kept one eye on Georgia. Alex finally managed to lure Georgia, Tash, and Emily to the dance floor for a fun rendition of "Girls Just Want to Have Fun," but once the music slowed, Tash and Emily partnered off and slow danced, so Belle and Alex swirled one another around the dance floor, while Georgia and Julie stood to the side, talking. Belle loved how easily Georgia fit in with her family. She'd almost forgotten Alex had first introduced them to one another.

Exhausted, Belle finally took a break from dancing and went to the table to grab a glass of water. Her mother wasn't far behind.

"Man, it's exhausting. I'm not as young as I once was." Julie sat down and sighed.

Belle agreed. She'd finally let her hair down, but the lead-up to the event and hosting the event itself was exhausting. Throwing dancing into the mix had tipped her over the edge.

"What a fun night—you've done so well, Belle."

Belle thanked her mum once again.

"How do you feel about Tash's news? I know you knew about it, but were you shocked when you found out?"

"Actually, she told me they were considering it, which was nice. She didn't have to. She wanted to know if I was happy if she used the girls' donor."

Julie's eyes widened. "Oh, I hadn't even thought about that. She did use the same donor? It's all a bit strange, isn't it?"

"I don't think it's strange. I think it's nice for the girls."

"Yes." Julie began to fiddle with the edge of the table-cloth. "I suppose so, It's just odd in a way."

Belle was frustrated that her mother had an opinion on the matter, but she saw Julie think it over, and then she said, "Actually, you're right. It is nice for the girls. I hope it's not strange for you, love."

"It would have been harder for me if it was Tash and Amanda, to be honest." Belle paused. "I've fully moved on now. I hadn't when she was dating Amanda. I'm genuinely happy for Tash, and Emily seems nice. I don't know her well, though."

"Well, that's great. It's nice when two people can co-parent well and have no issues with new partners. Maybe you and Emily will get to know one another, or maybe not. It's nice for the girls, regardless. And…Georgia… She's nice."

Belle smiled, acknowledging her mother's words.

"She wouldn't be the reason you've fully moved on?" Julie's eyebrows raised. She was trying to sound casual, but her question was anything but.

"Mum, she's straight!" Belle responded.

"Oh, is she, darling? I don't know these things. I don't think I have the—what is it?— Gay radar?"

"Gaydar. You certainly don't have gaydar. Georgia isn't gay."

"Mmm. Maybe not, but I've seen you looking at her."

"A gay woman can look at a straight woman as much as she wants. She isn't going to get her to change teams!" Belle laughed, exasperated. "I've never chased straight women, and I'm not going to make an exception for Georgia!"

"You were just a child when you and Tash got together, love. Of course you've never chased straight women. You've never had the chance."

Belle hated that her mother knew her so well. "Well, I've told you before, I'm not intending on dating while the girls are young. They've got enough instability in their lives with Tash."

"From where I'm standing, Tash is looking pretty stable." Julie nodded toward the dance floor where Tash and Emily were still slow dancing and looking like there was no one else in the room.

"Fair enough. I get it. Maybe one day I will date. I'll join an app some time. I'll definitely avoid straight women. They can only lead to heartbreak."

"Sometimes not following your heart can lead to heartbreak."

"Mum!" she exclaimed. "Where's Dad? Where's Alex? Surely you should go find them?"

Her mother laughed. "I just want to see you happy, darling. That girl seems to make you happy. But what would I know?"

"What would make me happy is for you to butt out of my romantic life—or lack of romantic life." Belle was grinning as she spoke as a signal to her mother that, while it wasn't helpful, she appreciated her mother's interest in her happiness. "I am happy, and I'm completely devoted to my girls. I don't really have time to focus on matters of the heart, anyway."

Her mother was serious again. "I had two daughters, too, and then they grew up and told me to butt out of their lives." She winked at Belle. "Your devotion to your children is something I admire. Just don't forget to look after yourself too. One day the girls will have lives of their own. It seems like it will be many years away, but you'll be surprised at how quickly things will change, honey."

Belle had to admit, even if only to herself, her mother probably had a point. Right now, in the thick of parenting, even if it was only half-time, it did seem like her days would always be about raising children, but she'd also seen how quickly the years had already passed in the girls' lives.

"I think you're right."

"What's that?" Belle's mother asked. "Did I just hear you say I'm right, or is my hearing playing tricks on me?" Belle playfully wacked her mother and laughed. Her mother feigned mock hurt, but then embraced her daughter, and agreed she would go to find Belle's father. Belle was secretly relieved that her mother's grilling would be finished for the evening.

*

"I'M EXHAUSTED," GEORGIA said at the end of the night, "but it was fabulous."

"It *was* fabulous," Tash said. "One of the best ones yet, I think, Annabelle."

"Thanks." Belle grinned, proud of her work. "I think I'll call a cab and head home."

"I can drive you," Georgia and Emily both said at the same time. Of course the two pregnant women were designated drivers. "Thank you, but I may as well go with Emily and Tash— they live closer."

Georgia screwed her face up. "I'm like ten minutes from you. Let me drive you."

"It's fine, I'll go with Emily and Tash," Belle insisted. "You'll get home faster."

Tash watched on as Georgia and Belle spoke, and then said to Belle, "Go with Georgia. That way she'll have company for the walk to the car." Belle wondered whether Tash really cared whether Georgia had company or not, or whether she, like Julie, thought that there was something between them. Belle rolled her eyes but agreed to head home in Georgia's car. It was pointless to argue any more.

Once they were driving home, Georgia said to Belle, "If the blood test on Monday goes well, they want me to have a scan the following week. Would you like to come with me? Play the role of the good wife?"

"You're pregnant now. I don't know if you need me there."

Georgia smiled. "I *want* you there."

In some way, Belle wanted to be there anyway. "I'm happy to go, but I really don't think you have to pretend to be in a relationship with me now. They're not going to take the baby off you now." Belle laughed at her own joke.

"Maybe not, but there's still a long journey to go. Anyway, I'd like you there, if you're happy to be. Next week, maybe email me some dates that work best for you the following week, and I'll make the appointment. Just remember, it's such early days, and my body has betrayed me for so long." Georgia's eyes filled with tears. "There's every chance this won't work out."

"True, but Dr. Cooper also said there's no reason you can't have a healthy pregnancy with a donor embryo. This is so exciting!"

"I'm trying not to get excited. I wish I was like Emily, at the twelve-week mark. Then I could relax much more.

But I'm so happy anyway."

"It'll be nice to have babies so close together," Belle said, and then shook her head, realising what she'd just said. "I suppose you aren't friends with Tash and Emily, so it doesn't matter." She couldn't believe she'd said anything that implied a family connection, even though the babies were created by the same sperm donor.

"I don't really have friends with babies. Maybe we will become friendlier. Or maybe not. But, the two babies share a donor, just like Cora and Ada. It's a modern family, in a strange way. So, it's kind of nice. They're due eight weeks apart."

Belle grinned as she got out of the car. "I love newborn cuddles, so I'm excited for the end of the year." As soon as she said it, she had an uncomfortable feeling—Georgia was carrying her biological child.

When she'd decided to donate her embryos, Belle had thought it made sense and was a nice thing to do—to help out a family and potentially give life to the embryos. She hadn't thought that an acquaintance would become the mother of her own biological child and that she would see the child grow up. She certainly hadn't thought that person would become one of her closest friends. While Georgia was pregnant, their friendship was safe, but Belle realised this was becoming dangerous. And whenever Georgia looked at her, really looked at her, Belle realised it was becoming more dangerous than she ever thought possible.

Chapter Seventeen

"AARGH, I'M SO nervous," Georgia said, and Belle noticed her hands were shaking.

"It's a scary time, the first scan."

Georgia screwed her face up. "Yeah. I just feel like it's taken me so long to get to this point."

"You've got a lot riding on it."

"And you too. I shouldn't forget that this impacts on you." Georgia grabbed Belle's hand and looked at her intently. "You're a big part of all of this. Without you, there is no this."

"It doesn't impact me as much as it impacts on you." But then she looked at Georgia, wondering what there was between them. Wondering what her role with the baby might end up being. Wondering whether they were friends, or more than friends. Wondering what on earth Georgia saw between them. Wondering if she was just an embryo donor going along for the pregnancy. Wondering why she was doing this to herself.

Again, she reminded herself she was simply an embryo donor in a fake relationship with a very straight friend. But, at the same time, she couldn't help feeling that her moments with Georgia were the most intimate moments she'd had in years. She couldn't help but think there was something in the way that Georgia looked at her. There was definitely something in the way she held her hand. But did it only mean something to Belle?

The nurse called them into the room, interrupting her thoughts. "We do a transvaginal ultrasound at this early stage," the nurse explained. "We can't see much with a belly ultrasound, but once you're twelve weeks and on-wards, that's how we'll do it."

"Okay," Georgia said anxiously. Once the nurse left the room, Georgia got ready, then sat up on the bed. "I'm so nervous, my hands are shaking." She held her hand out to Belle. Belle moved to the chair next to the bed and sat down, taking Georgia's hand. During the scan, they held hands.

The ultrasound technician moved the ultrasound wand around inside Georgia, looking at her uterus. She then stopped on a blob that resembled a baby if you squinted hard enough. "See that? That's your baby."

Georgia grinned and turned to Belle, who had tears in her eyes. "There's our baby," Georgia whispered. Belle felt so touched for the inclusion, and so confused.

The technician continued. "See the flicker just there? There?" She pointed at the flickering on the screen. Georgia nodded, clearly anticipating the explanation. "That's your baby's heartbeat. It's too soon for us to hear it, but we can see it. At the twelve-week mark, you should be able to hear it, all going well. But the fact we've got to this point is a very good sign."

Tears sprang to Georgia's eyes, but she was grinning. Belle was relieved.

They both had to rush to work straight after the scan, so said farewell, and Georgia gave Belle a hug. "Thanks for coming," she said. "I can't believe I have a baby in here." She pointed to her belly. "It's so surreal."

*

"OH, NIKKI, IT was so wonderful," Belle said to her friend on the phone after work that evening.

"I'm so happy for you. Or for Georgia. Or for you both."

"It really does feel strange, I'll tell you that much. I understand it's not my baby, I knew that going in, but it's all a bit weird."

"I guess it would be. It's not the usual way of things, is it?" Nikki pondered aloud.

"No, and that's why I was so keen to donate embryos. I wouldn't be a mother without the use of donor sperm. It's only due to the kindness of someone I didn't know that I have my girls. I wanted to give someone that too."

"Yes," Nikki responded, and then paused. "I guess it's just that the sperm donor is someone you don't know, while

Georgia—"

"Is quickly becoming one of my closest friends," Belle said.

"Oi!" said Nikki, laughing. "'One of' is fine, but, if you ever say *closest*, watch out."

"No, that won't happen. But I point it out, because I didn't expect to get this close to Georgia when I offered. It's not like we were close friends at the time. We've just become close because we've spent so much time together."

Nikki sighed. "Do you think it's your way of being close to the baby?"

Belle took some time to answer her, and then finally said, "No, I don't. Because we were becoming really close before I even knew she would get pregnant. We just really click. She's great."

"Maybe you need to find a girlfriend, then," Nikki said. "Maybe there's something missing in your life. Maybe that's why you've connected with her so much."

Belle rolled her eyes. "I've told you that I'm really happy single. For the first time in my life, I've got the opportunity to just be me. Just because you and Jason are all loved up doesn't mean the rest of us need that in our lives. I do not need a girlfriend, and I don't understand why you're even bringing that up, especially when she's straight."

"Just be careful, Belle." Now that was something they could both agree on.

*

"HERE WE ARE again," Georgia said on the day of the scan. This time they were not at the IVF clinic, but at an ultrasound place. "My hands are still shaking. I'm sure they haven't stopped since I first did that pee test." Georgia closed her eyes and exhaled, as if she was trying to calm herself down. "If all goes well, I think we should start to make the announcements."

"Well, it's really up to you," Belle said. She was always clear to ensure it was understood that Belle knew her place in this—embryo donor, full stop. She didn't want Georgia thinking she expected some rights over the baby, beyond what they had first discussed. Updates and photographs. Obviously, their friendship was blurring the lines a little, but Belle had to remind herself that friendships didn't always last forever. She wasn't going to hold Georgia ransom to a different kind of arrangement simply because they'd become friends.

When she and Tash had sat in this very waiting room, anxiously awaiting their scans for the girls, they'd discussed baby names, nursery décor, how much time to take off work, and who to tell and when. They had been completely there, together. In some ways sitting beside Georgia felt very different. In other ways, it felt just the same—the anticipation of a baby that was going to change their lives; the excitement and anxiety about what was to come.

A tall, young man called them in to the room. He introduced himself and explained the process. Within minutes, Georgia was up on the bed and the gel was being rubbed on her tummy. Up on the screen popped the image—a much more baby-like image than what had appeared weeks earlier. Soon, he tuned the sound in, and they could hear the baby's beating heart. Georgia instantly burst into tears, and that started Belle crying too. She looked down at Georgia through her tears, and Georgia grinned, then reached up and wiped away one of Belle's tears.

"Relieved?" the ultrasound technician asked. The two women nodded in unison, grinning through their tears.

"It's been a complicated path to get here," Georgia confessed openly. "And now I'm carrying Belle's embryo," she explained, and then reached to hold Belle's hand.

"Oh, I see a lot of couples that do that," he said. "It's nice that it's worked out, and that you're now becoming parents."

"Oh I'm not—" Belle started to tell him that she wasn't Georgia's partner, but Georgia spoke over the top of her.

"She's not a first-time parent," Georgia said. "This is just our first together." Georgia smiled at Belle, but she frowned in confusion back at her. They were no longer at the IVF clinic. There was no reason to pretend anymore.

At lunch, Belle asked her why she'd done that. Georgia shrugged. "It *is* our first child together. I don't know, to be honest. It's complicated, isn't it?"

"It's complicated, but it needn't be. I donated an embryo to you." When she said it like that, it sounded simple, but it felt anything but. "I'm not this baby's mother."

"No, I will be," Georgia said, "but what role do you want?"

Belle sighed. As she spoke, slowly, she shook her head. "I don't know. I said photos and updates to you in the early days, but obviously we're closer now than we were then." Georgia nodded, but didn't say anything, so Belle continued to speak. "An aunty type of role, I suppose? But with no expectations from you. This is your child."

"Thank you. You're one of my best friends now. I love spending time with you, and I hope you'll be a big part of our lives."

Belle smiled, relieved. That was what she wanted, but it hurt, even to admit that to herself.

Georgia continued. "Our children will be biological siblings too. Maybe I can babysit your girls, or you can babysit my kid? Let them have some sleepovers together."

Belle silently wondered whether she and Georgia could have sleepovers too. She kicked herself for thinking it. Things were complicated enough without her getting a crush on Georgia. Her mother and Nikki were right—she needed to tread carefully. She simply responded, "I'm so happy for you."

As they paid for their lunches, Georgia turned to Belle. "Who do you want to tell?"

"Just Alex, Mum, and Dad," Belle said.

"Not Tash?"

"Maybe I'll wait until later on. There's no rush." Belle decided to wait until the twenty-week scan but didn't want to say that to Georgia in case it worried her that they shouldn't be excited yet.

*

THAT EVENING, SHE invited her parents and sister over for a barbeque dinner. It was her week with the girls, and Belle often had the family over when the girls were with her. After dinner, the girls went to the lounge room to play, while the adults stayed at the table. Belle was nervous but just blurted it out.

"You know how we had embryos left over?"

Everyone nodded, and Julie said, "Oh my God, you're pregnant?" Alex looked knowingly at Belle. She knew that Belle had intended to donate the embryos to Georgia, so would have put two and two together.

Belle gave a crooked grin in response to her mother's question. "No, I'm not pregnant. I donated the embryos."

Her father looked surprised. "You donated them? To a couple, or to science?"

"To a family. Well, a single mother, actually." Julie and Clive looked at one another to check each other's reactions. They both nodded apprehensively, clearly waiting for further information. "Do you remember Georgia?"

Julie audibly gasped. "Oh, honey," she said, clearly concerned. She shook her head. "I'm not so sure that's a good idea."

"Good idea or not, it's done," Belle said flippantly. "And I'm happy with it."

"Well, that's...good." Her mother always panicked first, blurted out her feelings, but would inevitably be supportive.

"What do you mean done, though? Done as in you have an agreement, or done as in..." Her father blushed as he spoke.

"Done as in done, and not only done. Georgia's pregnant."

"Oh, lovely!" Belle's mother spoke up. "Another grandchild."

"Well, that's the thing," Belle said. "It's Georgia's child, not mine. I've donated the embryo to Georgia, so it won't actually be your grandchild."

Clive fiddled with his placemat, and then said, "Well, it's as much our grandchild as Cora and Ada, isn't it?"

Belle shook her head in response. "It won't be. Think of it as if I had a baby and adopted it out. Embryo donation is a bit similar, except that Georgia's doing the pregnancy part too. If I adopted out a baby, it wouldn't be your grandchild."

"It actually would," Clive said. "Biologically and as far as your mother and I are concerned, it would be. Anyway, if you're right, and it's not our grandchild, will we even get to meet the baby?"

Julie had remained silent during this exchange, but Belle could tell she was thinking something. Finally, she spoke up, directing her comment to her husband. "The thing is, love, Georgia is that lovely girl we met at the Gala. She's a friend of both Annabelle and Alexandra."

"Right," Clive said, clearly exasperated. "So we'll get to meet the child, is that what you're saying?"

Julie nodded slowly. "I expect so." She then turned to Belle. "Darling, it's not that I'm not happy for Georgia. I am. It's just that… Oh, darling, I saw the way you look at her." She gave her a look that screamed sympathy and worry. "I told you not to get your heart broken, and now…" Julie's voice was muffled, and Belle saw tears in her eyes. She suddenly wished she'd talked to her mother alone, and especially so when she noticed Alex's eyes on her.

"Huh?" Alex said. "You haven't got a crush on Georgia?"

Belle took a moment too long to respond. "Georgia's straight," she said.

"That wasn't the question," Alex said pointedly.

Belle shrugged. "She's just a friend," she mumbled in response.

"Seriously?" Alex said. "Are you okay?" She looked really concerned.

"I don't have a crush on her. Mum's imagining things. I'm happily single. I like Georgia, she's a great girl, but I'm not looking for a girlfriend. I had one of those, had the family of my dreams, and look where that got me." Belle was fighting back the tears but knew her voice was choked up.

"We just want you to be happy," Julie said, "and getting some girl pregnant when you're not in a relationship… Well, I don't know about that, I have to be honest."

Alex and Belle both laughed.

"It's not like I had sex with her and got her up the duff, Mum! God, you sound like the mother of a seventeen-year-old boy, not the mother of an adult lesbian who kindly donated her embryos she no longer required."

Even Clive started to laugh, and finally Julie, realising the craziness of the situation, also joined in. "You're right, darling, you're absolutely right. I just worry about my girls and their happiness. If donating your embryos to Georgia makes you happy, then who am I to judge?"

"To be fair," Alex started, "I think Belle decided to donate to Georgia when they weren't friends. Just acquaintances."

Belle nodded her agreement.

"Maybe the friendship has complicated things, but it's not like she donated embryos to Georgia hoping she'd fall in love with her."

"Absolutely not," Belle said, relieved her little sister was sticking up for her. "Not in the slightest. Whatever you think you saw between Georgia and me—which, by the way, will go nowhere because she's straight and I'm happily single—well, whatever that was, it wasn't there when I offered to donate to her. And maybe I wouldn't have donated to her if I thought there was something there."

Julie sat back in her chair and sighed audibly. "So you're having regrets, love?"

"Not at all. I'm thrilled for Georgia."

"I did think she should tell you about all of this early on," Alex said pointedly.

Julie raised an eyebrow. "You knew about this?"

"Not that they'd transferred the embryo, or that Georgia was pregnant. I knew she was considering it. I rang her and said, 'Tell Mum and Dad.'"

Belle rolled her eyes but was bemused—her sister, ever

the tattletale. She spoke up, "Yes, and I said that you'd support me no matter what. After all, they were my embryos, and I'm an adult."

"What about Tash?" Clive asked, his brow creasing. "Does she know? Because they're her embryos too."

"No. When she and Emily started trying for a baby, she signed the embryos over to me. She told me I could make all decisions about them. I'll have to tell her eventually, since the baby will be a full bio sibling of the girls, but maybe I'll wait until around the twenty-week mark. Just to be sure."

"Are you sure?" her mother asked. "You don't think you owe it to her to tell her sooner rather than later?"

Belle appreciated her mother's confusion. She had gone back and forth on the matter herself—who had rights over the embryos? But all she could remember was how flippant Tash had been, that Belle would have all rights and responsibilities. Tash had wanted to sever her responsibilities over the embryos, and as far as Belle was concerned, that meant she had also severed her rights. Deep down, Belle was reluctant to have the conversation, because she felt guilty. She realised now she probably should have told Tash before she agreed to the donation, but she didn't know what she could do about it, so it was easier to just let it go.

"Oh, this is all so confusing," Clive said, and everyone around the table agreed.

*

THE NEXT MONTH passed quickly. Belle was busy at work, which always helped, and when she wasn't working, she was spending time with the girls. She caught up with Nikki regularly, though less frequently than she had before Nikki and Jason had moved in together. Belle and Georgia talked most days, even if it was just a check-in text, but neither of them initiated many catch ups. Every Wednesday, Georgia sent a 'bump' photo to Belle, for 'Bump Day'—the day in the middle of the working week. Belle looked forward to her Bump Day photos and had stored them up in a photo album on her phone.

She was both happy and a little anxious that they weren't spending much time together in the second trimester. In the first trimester, they'd caught up so frequently, it was hard for Belle to focus her thoughts on anything but Georgia and the baby. But since the twelve-week scan, they'd only caught up a handful of times. This didn't mean that Georgia wasn't on Belle's mind—she was, fairly constantly—but it felt different to when she saw her all the time. And now, at the sixteen-week mark, they were catching up for dinner on the Friday night. Belle was looking forward to checking in with her.

Friday night seemed to come around quickly, and Belle walked into the Turkish restaurant wearing purple silky wide-leg trousers and a flowing, silky white top to match. It was a new designer she'd found out about through her work, and she was enjoying wearing lots of different colours. She noticed Georgia at the back of the restaurant, wearing a blue dress. Her bump was growing beautifully, though much smaller than Belle had been when she was this pregnant. "You look great." Georgia was glowing. Her olive skin had developed a shine, and she was grinning. She really appeared to be the definition of pregnancy glow.

"Thank you," Georgia said. "You look great yourself. I love this outfit."

Belle explained about the new designer and the various outfits. "I even have these incredible lilac harem pants, but I figured I couldn't wear them here," she said, referring to the Turkish restaurant. They both laughed and then got busy ordering the banquet dinner.

"Special occasion?" the waiter asked, and the women shook their heads. They both agreed the banquet was the best value and they got to enjoy many different things off the menu. The waiter agreed. "It's my favourite too," he said.

They started with breads and dips and made their way through to main course of pides, zucchini balls, vegetables, and salads, and concluded their dinner with desserts. During dinner, they caught up on work, their friends and family, and what Cora and Ada had been up to. "As of this afternoon, Tash and Emily have the girls, and so I'm going out with Lucy tomorrow afternoon, and then a quiet Sunday at home. I might catch a movie with Nikki during the week."

"You seem busy," Georgia said.

"Fairly busy, I often am on my child-free week," Belle said. "But nothing too exciting. Just catching up with everyone. I don't spend a lot of time with Lucy, but it'll be nice to have drinks with her tomorrow afternoon. What are your plans?"

"I'm going over to Jo's. She's my cousin. She's having a barbeque tomorrow afternoon. If you and Lucy end up feeling like popping in, just text me. I'm sure you have plenty to do, though."

"Thanks, that's kind of you. I think we'll catch up in the city, though, and I'm not sure what we'll end up doing. But I'll certainly be in touch if we find we're at a loose end. It would be nice to meet your cousins after all you've talked about them."

"You and Jo would get on like a house on fire. Jo's lots of fun, and I think you'd really enjoy her company and she'd love you."

"Well, if I don't get to meet her tomorrow, I'd love to meet her sometime soon."

*

THE NEXT AFTERNOON, Belle met Lucy in the city. They met up at a bar and spent the afternoon chatting about work and life. Belle told Lucy that she'd donated embryos to a friend, though she didn't tell Lucy who the friend was. They discussed the pregnancy and how everything was going. Lucy told Belle about a new job she was applying for. "Oh, would you be reporting to Bill Jacobs?"

"Yes, do you know him?" Lucy asked in response. Belle and Lucy always loved talking shop and sharing their insights into the fashion world.

"I did an internship for him when I was studying, and then years later I did a consultancy project for him. He's a really nice guy, but put it this way—he's dated nearly every assistant he's ever had. You're lucky you're not applying for a PA role with him."

Lucy said, "Thanks very much! If I get this job, I'll now be watching as his PA takes minutes in all his meetings, seeing if she's sharing lingering glances at him." Lucy and Belle kept talking and laughing, and they were still laughing when Kate, Lucy's wife, turned up at about four o'clock, with a friend of hers. "This is Riley," she said, introducing the tall woman beside her.

"Sit down," Belle said kindly. She was a little

disappointed. She had been enjoying catching up with Lucy, but she assumed Kate's arrival marked the end of their one-on-one time. "We've been sharing a bottle of wine, but we're nearly at the end of it. Shall I get us something more?"

Riley shook her head. "Let me. Are you happy with the wine you're drinking, or would you like something else?" They placed their orders for more of the same, and Riley came back juggling wine and beer on a small tray.

Soon enough, the four women were chatting, laughing, and relaxed. It was very clear to Belle that Riley was gay, and there was no denying Riley was good looking. Belle couldn't help but wonder if it was a set-up of some sort. She couldn't believe it—she'd told Lucy and Kate she wasn't keen to date, and they knew she wasn't a casual sex type of girl. Then again, she could be completely wrong, and it was merely a catch up between two groups of friends in the city. She figured she shouldn't analyse it, and just enjoy her afternoon with three fun women. At any rate it was nice to be surrounded by gay women for a change. They shared stories and talked about books and movies they'd recently enjoyed.

A few drinks in, Belle was really starting to feel the effects of the alcohol. She was feeling relaxed, happy, and enjoying the afternoon. Suddenly Lucy and Kate started gathering up their things. "We're going to head off now—we have a dinner party to get to."

Belle started to protest, and then they added, "Riley has no plans this evening; we thought the two of you could hang out." Belle rolled her eyes. It was clearly a set-up—a set-up she had no interest in. She was enjoying Riley's company though, and she needed more gay friends, so she ended up agreeing to stay.

As Lucy and Kate left the bar, Riley looked very pleased. "Would you like an early dinner? Soak up some of the alcohol?" she asked. Belle realised she was actually hungry, so she agreed and the two of them strolled past various restaurants, looking at the menus. They settled on a little Japanese place and ordered up sushi and various teppanyaki dishes. Although it was awkward initially, they began to really bounce off one another. "Where are you off to after here?" Riley asked, her intent clear.

"Off to bed, I think," Belle said innocently, but the response raised Riley's eyebrows.

"And are you interested in company? I'd prefer to be direct, not beat around the bush," Riley said.

Belle appreciated that she was so upfront. "I don't really do that," she confessed. "It's not you; it's me."

"That's a shame," Riley admitted, and Belle couldn't help but be flattered. "You're a beautiful woman."

Belle blushed. "Thank you, and you're very good looking, yourself." Belle wasn't saying it just to appease Riley. She was certain anyone would find Riley attractive. She didn't feel the chemistry with Riley that she felt with Georgia, but she certainly appreciated her looks. And then she wondered why on earth she was comparing Georgia to Riley when one was straight and one was gay.

After they paid the bill, Belle excused herself to go to the bathroom. Once alone in the bathroom, she looked at herself in the mirror and fluffed her hair up. She looked hard at herself—visibly tipsy, and yet sober enough to have a clear head. She pondered the proposition Riley had put on the table. She wasn't a casual sex girl, but really, why was that? She'd spent nearly two decades in a relationship with Tash, so of course it hadn't been an option back then. Since then, she'd wanted to be the stable person in her kids' lives while Tash had had all the fun. But, now? Tash was now stable, or at least, it appeared that way. Maybe it was time she let her hair down and enjoyed herself, and maybe it would be just this once, or maybe she'd decide there was something there. Perhaps Riley could be a nice distraction from Georgia. Maybe Riley could help take her mind off their friendship, the pregnancy, and ultimately, her growing attraction for Georgia. A very dangerous growing attraction for Georgia. By the time Belle left the restroom, she had made her mind up.

"Would you like to come to my place for coffee?" Belle said to Riley as she reached the table. Riley looked like she'd just been told she'd won the lottery, and Belle had to admit to herself how nice it was to have that effect on someone.

The two of them shared a taxi to Belle's home, and Belle made coffees while Riley stood in the kitchen talking to her. They made their way to the couch and chatted while sipping coffees. Belle placed her coffee down on the coaster on the coffee table, and Riley followed her lead. She then lent forward and gently kissed Belle, gradually building into a more passionate kiss. It was pleasant, she thought. Nice enough, though pleasant wasn't the word she wanted to use to describe a kiss from the second woman she'd ever kissed. Belle found herself thinking about how Riley tasted like a mix of strong coffee, beer, and red wine.

Over time, their kissing heated up, and Belle responded more than she thought she might initially. So, when Riley suggested they move to the bedroom, Belle was definitely happy to oblige. It felt wonderful to be touched after so long, and her body responded over and over. Afterwards, they lay in one another's arms, chatting. "That was pretty fun," Belle admitted.

"Would you like to do it again another time? Would you like to see one another again?"

"I'm not sure—I'm just out of a fairly complicated thing," she said, stretching the truth a little. Two years post-breakup was hardly 'just out,' but she figured it was best. "So, it's definitely not you and definitely not because of what we just did—that was fantastic. Really fantastic—but

I'm not sure if I'm in the headspace for anything bigger right now."

Riley nodded.

Belle knew her hesitation wasn't about Tash. Georgia was the main reason she was saying no. Belle wanted to get through the remainder of her pregnancy and work out her role in the baby's life before finding someone else and complicating matters anymore. It was all confusing enough. Riley seemed like a great girl, and Belle was grateful that she'd now officially moved on from the 'Belle and Tash' relationship, but she certainly wasn't ready to plunge into something new. It was the most complicated time for that. She wasn't an asshole, though, so she said, "It's getting late, so please feel free to spend the night." It would be nice to be cuddled, and maybe they could have a lazy Sunday morning in bed. Repeat it all again one last time.

Riley pondered the offer. "It's not that late—it's only ten thirty, but it would be nice to have some company overnight. And don't worry, I know what it is and what it isn't." With that, she reached over and started kissing Belle again, and as the kisses heated up, hands went everywhere. Riley stopped kissing Belle's mouth and began kissing her neck, and eventually moved down her body, trailing her lips and tongue all over every inch of Belle. As her body started to respond again, Belle wondered if she was crazy saying no to Riley simply due to circumstances. She was enjoying Riley getting busy between her legs when her phone on the bedside shrilly interrupted. She glanced at the phone and saw Georgia's name pop up. Georgia rang often enough, but never at 11:00 p.m. "I have to get this," Belle said. Riley either didn't hear, or didn't care, and kept going.

"Hello?" Georgia started speaking down the phone rapidly.

"Belle, sorry to ring you so late. Did I wake you?"

"No, I was still awake."

"I'm at the hospital."

"Are you okay?" Belle was panicked. Riley suddenly stopped what she was doing.

Georgia started sobbing down the phone. "I'm bleeding. They want me to stay in tonight, and they're going to scan me and see what's going on."

"Oh my God, I'll come straight up," Belle said. "Which

hospital?" It was sobering news, and Belle suddenly stopped feeling the effects of the wine.

Riley sat up from between Belle's legs and suddenly spoke. "Oh, crap. You okay? I can go, if you need to go to the hospital. I don't need to stay." Belle cringed as Riley's voice echoed down the phone.

Georgia was silent, and then spoke. "Belle, don't worry if you have company. Jo's here with me." Belle thought she sounded annoyed, but maybe she was just anxious.

"It's fine," Belle responded. "I'll be straight up. I want to be there."

As Belle hung up, Riley asked, "Everything okay?"

"It's my friend… She's bleeding, and pregnant." Belle teared up as she spoke.

"Oh crap," Riley said. "Very far along?"

"Sixteen weeks." Belle's voice was barely audible, and she felt like she couldn't breathe.

"Let's call a cab. We can go together. I can go home after we get to the hospital."

"Are you sure?" Belle asked, and Riley said she was. Belle called a cab, then threw jeans and a hoodie on, looking very different to the girl that Riley had met hours earlier. "Cute," Riley said, clearly impressed, but the compliment fell flat for Belle. She was now kicking herself that she'd even gone home with Riley. She was clearly a nice woman, and they had enough chemistry, but it just didn't feel right. In the cab, she looked at Riley and said, "I'm sorry."

Riley didn't seem to mind. "It's okay. Your friend's health is more important than a sleepover. We can take a raincheck."

"No." Belle looked down at her lap, avoiding Riley's eye contact. "About everything. That this was a once-off."

"Oh," Riley said. "Well, if you ever do want a rain-check, you'll let me know?" Riley wouldn't let Belle pay her part of the cab fare when she exited the cab. Belle appreciated her kindness. "Hope your friend's baby is okay," Riley said. "And here's my number if you get the time to update me on your friend, or if you're ever keen on that raincheck." With that, she thrust a piece of paper into the palm of Belle's hand.

Belle flew to the elevator and pressed the up button, and then gave up and raced up the stairs. She was puffing when she got to the nurse's desk. "I'm here to visit Georgia Reid. She called."

The nurse rustled her papers, finally giving up and typing Georgia's name into the computer. "Room three, down the left hall." She pointed.

Georgia was lying in her bed, next to a short woman with short dark curly hair—clearly Georgia's cousin Jo. On the other side, a nurse was fixing an IV drip. "Hi, I'm Belle," Belle said as she entered the room, directing her introduction to Jo. She caught Georgia's eye and moved toward the bed gave her a kiss on the cheek. "You okay?"

Georgia nodded but looked so frightened it nearly broke Belle's heart.

"I'm Jo, Georgia's cousin. She's just getting a drip because she's very dehydrated. I promise I was looking after her, but..." Jo paused. "I don't actually know why she's dehydrated. She was at my house and went to the bathroom and came back looking incredibly pale. She had quite a bit of blood. We came straight up. They're going to take her for a scan soon."

Belle appreciated Jo's rundown of events. Georgia

didn't look like she was in a position to talk.

"Are you staying?" Jo asked Belle. When Belle confirmed she would stay as long as the hospital allowed her, Jo turned to Georgia. "I might go home and pack you a bag, then? And I'll bring up some drive through coffees on the way back?"

"How long do you think she'll be in hospital?" Belle asked.

Jo shrugged. "I suppose it depends on the scan results. But I'm dying for a coffee, anyway, and it'd be nice to get her some PJs or something." Belle agreed, and after taking coffee orders, Jo disappeared. The nurse called the wardsman to take them up to the ultrasound room.

"I'm so pleased Jo was with you," Belle said to Georgia while they were waiting. "I'm so pleased you had someone to look after you."

"I'm so nervous," Georgia said. "I knew twelve weeks wasn't some magic green light, but gosh, I really thought…" Tears began to spill out of her eyes. Belle embraced her and just held her. She didn't want to tell Georgia it would all be okay because she didn't know herself.

The doctor on duty was a friendly, young woman, and she did the ultrasound herself. She talked through it. "Your baby is fine," she said, and relief instantly flooded through Belle's body. "The issue seems to be the position of the placenta. It might just have been bumped. Right now it's at the entrance of your cervix. It's still early in your pregnancy, so it might move. If it doesn't move, we'll diagnose it as placenta previa, and you'll need a C-section."

"But the baby will be okay?" Georgia asked, clearly very anxious.

"This baby is looking very healthy. It's a big baby and might just be putting some pressure on the placenta. The placenta is in the wrong place, but they are a little mobile at this point. What I want to do is see you again in a few days, and then again in a month. But for now, I'd encourage you to get some rest, avoid sex, and relax a little."

"Will I go home tonight?"

"We've already admitted you, and it's getting late. I think the best thing is for you to stay up here tonight, and then go home tomorrow. Rest as much as you can."

Georgia looked pale. Belle wondered if it was because

she was dehydrated. "Doctor, apparently Georgia is quite dehydrated. Are the two related?"

The doctor shook her head. "No, but dehydration is common in pregnancy, particularly if you've had morning sickness, or been off your food. Are you okay?"

"I throw up occasionally, but I'm probably not eating enough," Georgia said.

The doctor gave her a lecture on nutrition and made an appointment for Georgia with a dietician at the hospital. "I'll make them for the same day as the re-scan, so you can get both done at once." The doctor wrote appointments down on a card.

Not long after they returned to the ward, Jo entered the room with three takeaway cups of coffee. "Cappuccino." She handed a cup to Belle. "And lattes for us," she said, handing a cup to Georgia.

"Thank you, this is great," Belle said, having her first sip. "It's been a long night." Georgia shot her a pointed look, and Belle remembered that just hours ago, she'd had Riley in her bed.

"It sure has. I'm exhausted," Jo agreed. "I was up early

getting the barbeque ready, then being social queen, and now, it's almost 1:00 a.m."

"I'm so sorry, guys." Georgia filled Jo in about the diagnosis.

"You, rest?" Jo raised her eyebrows with a grin on her face. "I'd love to see that."

Belle looked concerned. "Can you take it easy at home?"

Georgia paused for a moment, clearly thinking, then spoke. "I guess I can take the week off work. I can just let the laundry mount up for the week."

"And who is going to cook for you? The doctor said you need to eat," Belle said.

"I can cook for her, and drop meals over," Jo said. "She'll be right."

Belle wasn't convinced. "I have a spare room. How about you stay at my house? I'm kid-free this week. We can reassess after the scan on Thursday."

Georgia looked at Jo who spoke up. "Well, it makes sense if you're happy to. And if you've got Netflix and chocolate, Belle, I'm sure Georgia will be happy."

Belle nodded. "I definitely do have Netflix. And cable too. And I can get chocolate for her."

"Well, then, I guess that's set," Jo said. "If you're happy?" Belle was worried Georgia's might pride might mean she said no, but she readily agreed.

"Happy," she said. "It'll be reassuring to have the company to be honest. Oh, but Oscar…"

"I can take Oscar to my house," Jo said, "if you need me to. You know I love cats."

"Okay, thanks," Georgia said.

Jo spoke up. "Okay. Well for now, I'll stay here, and you go home and get some sleep," she said to Belle. Then, turning to Georgia, she said, "Sounds like you'll be discharged tomorrow, so then you can go home with Belle, but if you need me at all, I'm only a phone call away. I'll walk Belle to her car. You try and sleep." Georgia asked Jo to take her to the bathroom. It was clear that Georgia was very anxious. Jo took the pyjamas in with her, and when they came out, Georgia looked clearly exhausted, but much more comfortable than she had in the dress she'd had on all day.

"Let's head to the car," Jo said.

"Actually, I took a cab."

"Why?" Georgia asked, frowning in confusion a little.

"Oh, I had a few drinks."

Georgia shot a curious look at Belle but didn't say anything.

"I'll walk you to the taxi rank?" Jo asked and Belle nodded.

"Good night," Belle said, and kissed her friend's forehead.

"Night," Georgia said with a sleepy smile and lay back on the bed.

As they walked toward the taxi rank, Jo asked her if she was okay getting a cab home. "I'm sure Georgia's fine if you want me to drop you home."

"You must be exhausted. Go up to the room and try to get some sleep. I'll be fine. I'm so pleased you were with her today."

Jo smiled and then looked at Belle. "Thanks to you for donating the embryos to Georgia. She's the happiest I've ever seen her."

Belle smiled proudly, so happy that she had a part in

Georgia's happiness. "I wanted to donate my embryos—I just didn't realise that I'd be donating to someone who would become my friend."

"Well, I'm pleased you did, and I'm so happy she's staying with you. I only have a small place, and the bedrooms are upstairs, which probably isn't ideal for her. She seems so anxious."

"Probably more anxious than the situation requires, but given the circumstances…"

"Exactly. Oh, Belle, I don't know if she's told you everything, but this has been such a long time coming. I seriously think if she was encouraged to be on bedrest for the rest of the pregnancy, she would be."

"I think I have the full story—from starting with Michael, to using a sperm donor, and now the embryo donation. I really feel for her."

Jo agreed. As they got to the door of the hospital, Jo embraced Belle. "So lovely to finally meet you. Georgia has told me how amazing you are—non-stop—but it's nice to finally meet you. I'd love to have you and the girls over sometime, but let's get through this hiccup first."

"Well, you're welcome to visit Georgia any time this week."

Jo grinned, and then hugged Belle. "Welcome to the family," she said, and Belle grinned.

"I'm not really part of the family; I'm just donating to the family."

"Listen, the Reid family welcomes people who have come to dinner once. You've donated a new member to the family. I think you're part of the family, whether you like it or not. Anyway, you better get home, otherwise it'll be daylight before you do."

Belle hopped into a taxi, waved goodbye to Jo, and grinned the whole way home. Jo had made her feel so welcome, and she was relieved that Georgia was coming to stay. Belle sleepily decided she'd work from home during the week to keep an eye on Georgia. So exhausted, she fell asleep instantly once she finally climbed into bed.

She didn't wake until late—about ten—but she quickly ate breakfast, showered, and dressed. As she was throwing on clothes for the day, she noticed her discarded clothes from the evening before with Riley lying at the foot of her bed. What a surreal twenty-four hours she'd just experienced. Picking up a woman and having a one-nighter had not been on her agenda for the weekend. Seriously, it was bizarre. She'd kissed the second person she'd ever kissed and been intimate with the only person other than her partner of nearly twenty years. And if that wasn't crazy enough, she'd then made a mad dash to the hospital in the middle of the night and was about to get a new 'housemate.' Her whole world had changed since Georgia had innocently asked what her plans for the weekend were. The quiet Sunday she'd envisaged was getting upturned by Georgia moving in, though Belle supposed they would have a quiet afternoon sitting on the lounge suite talking.

After a quick tidy of the house, Belle drove to the hospital. Georgia was lying in the bed, but she had more colour in her face than she'd had the night before. Jo wasn't in the room, and Belle figured she might have gone home to sleep. The drip had been removed. "IV is gone?" Belle asked happily. Surely that was a good sign.

"Yes. The nurse just finished taking it out. Apparently, things are looking good, and I'm heading home. Jo could have driven me home." Georgia had an apologetic tone in her voice, clearly worried Belle had wasted the trip up. "She's just gone in search of coffee." Georgia then spoke again. "Ugh, listen to me, calling your place *home*. I promise I'm not moving in for good. I've always called places home when they're where I'm staying—hotels, friend's houses. Sorry."

"Don't be," Belle said, shaking her head. "I'm happy to have a housemate."

The two women grinned at one another, and Jo came bustling in. "Oh, God, you're here, Belle. If only someone had texted me, I could have got you a coffee too. But God, the whole thing was crazy. The queue was a mile long. You're best off avoiding it, unless you're desperate." She was looking at Belle. "And I *was* desperate."

Jo handed a takeaway coffee to Georgia, who looked at the cup, and then spoke in Belle's direction. "You know I'd given up coffee during the pregnancy? This is my third since last night. Jo is a really bad influence on me."

Jo playfully wacked her cousin. "Doesn't help that we were both exhausted," Jo justified.

"I think I drank coffee through my entire pregnancy with Ada. I tried to give it up, but I had Cora keeping me up at night. There was no way. I certainly reduced my consumption. It was a token effort." She didn't want Georgia to feel she had to justify her eating and drinking to her. "Just remember, there's no such thing as a perfect pregnancy. Even the doctors say everything in moderation."

Once Georgia was discharged, Belle, Georgia, and Jo walked to the carpark. Jo deposited Georgia's bag into the boot of Belle's car and then said goodbye.

At home, Belle settled Georgia into the guest room and gave her a lesson on the remote control and various television options. "Have you called in sick for tomorrow?" Georgia nodded, and Belle then told her that she planned to work from home. "I don't know though, whether you'd prefer to be alone, or have me at your beck and call?"

"Can you even work well from home? What's your week like this week?"

"I think I can, but I might go in tomorrow to check out things, bring a few things home. Even if I do go into the office, I'll not be far, so just call me if you need anything. Do you want some books or anything?"

"Actually, Jo got me some off my nightstand, so I should be kept busy enough between that and the TV."

That evening, after dinner, they sat watching mindless television. Belle's phone rang at about 8:00 p.m. Belle apologised, and answered the phone, talking as quietly as she could, while Georgia continued watching the program.

"Hello?"

"Oh, hi, it's Riley."

"Oh…hi…" Belle blushed instantly.

"I got your number off Lucy. I know I gave you my number, but I didn't get yours." Belle was going to give Lucy a piece of her mind when she saw her next. "I hope you don't think I'm a creepy stalker," Riley laughed. "I mostly wanted to catch up and see how your friend was."

As Riley mentioned Georgia, Belle glanced at her, actively watching the television. "She's okay. The baby's fine." Georgia glanced at Belle, but then looked back to the television quickly.

"That's great."

"It is great. Thanks."

There was awkward silence between the two of them; then Riley spoke up. "So, I really enjoyed last night. I was sorry it was cut short, though I totally understand you wanted to be with your friend. I wondered if we could take two. I know you said it was a once-off, but maybe you woke up smiling this morning." There was a flirty undertone to Riley's voice.

Belle noticed that Georgia was engrossed in her television show, so responded, quietly. "Sorry, Riley. I meant what I said, I don't usually do that, and I'm not actually looking for anything. It was fun, but I really am not in the right space for that."

When she looked back at Georgia, she was watching Belle, not the screen.

*

THE NEXT EVENING, over dinner, Georgia brought the topic up. "When I rang you from the hospital, you had company…" she said, placing her fork down on her plate.

Belle paused before responding, and then figured Georgia wouldn't care—they weren't in a relationship together, after all. She slowly nodded. "I did."

"Was it Lucy?"

Belle considered using the 'out' Georgia was giving her, but she'd learnt the hard way how much dishonesty could impact on relationships, and she included important friendships in that category, so instead she shook her head. "It was a friend of Lucy's, someone I met through her."

"Ah." Georgia was silent for a moment. Belle briefly looked away, but it seemed that was enough for Georgia to draw her own conclusion. "And that was her on the phone last night?" Belle nodded, again.

"Are you and her…?" She used her pointer finger, shaking it back and forth.

Belle shook her head in response. "No, we're not." Georgia simply bit her lip in response. Belle worried that Georgia might think she did this type of thing often and didn't know whether explaining that made it sound better or worse. It would certainly implicate her, so if there was any chance Georgia didn't suspect correctly what had gone on, it was best left. The awkwardness that was suddenly felt between them meant Belle suspected Georgia did indeed know. If it were Nikki, she would want all the goss and demand Belle tell her every sordid detail. Perhaps she and Georgia simply didn't know one another well enough for that, or perhaps there was another reason the mood had turned awkward rather than fun and full of teasing. Was she just reading something into it?

Belle stood up. "I'll do the dishes, then." She quickly busied herself clearing the dinner plates.

*

THANKFULLY THE AWKWARDNESS seemed to be short-lived. The week passed, with Belle working between home and the office, cooking dinner for the two of them, and generally pampering Georgia as much as possible. When she wasn't with her, she couldn't stop thinking about her, and when she was with her, she basked in every moment they spent together. Being together was just easy. It was fun. They made one another laugh, and even when they weren't talking, it was still comfortable. Just being side by side felt right.

The only discomfort Belle felt was wondering if the

chemistry she sensed between them was mutual. Surely, she couldn't be wrong about something she felt so strongly? And yet, because Georgia was pregnant—with her biological child, mind you—Belle was particularly hesitant to even suggest there could be something between them in case that sent Georgia running. Plus, Georgia was straight. She had never mentioned interest in females, and so Belle had to tread carefully not to get her heart broken. She'd sworn off women long ago, and nothing was going to change that— certainly not the beautiful, but very straight woman carrying her biological child and currently living with her. She was still happily single, devoted to her daughters, and she kept reminding herself she wasn't looking for a relationship. Riley was on offer if she really needed someone. An easy, comfortable friendship was something rare, and she didn't need to do anything to ruin that, especially with Georgia's baby on the way.

One evening, as they were eating dinner, Belle asked Georgia if she was finding out the sex of the baby. She usually asked this question of her pregnant friends early on but had kept avoiding the topic waiting for a 'safe' moment in the pregnancy. Now it seemed that the baby would be okay—the only questions that seemed up in the air were what type of birth Georgia could have, if she could work up until the birth, and whether or not she needed to be on bed rest.

"I'm only asking because you're nearly seventeen weeks; they might be able to see at the scan tomorrow," Belle explained.

Georgia crinkled her nose. "I don't think I will."

"Really?" Belle was surprised. Most people seemed to find out these days.

"I'm enjoying wondering. I keep changing what I think." Georgia had a shy smile on her face.

"What do you think it is?"

"A girl. But before, I was adamant it was a boy. Now I'm pretty sure it will be a girl. Who knows what I will think later?" She smiled. "What do you think it is?"

Whenever Belle had pictured her third child, it was another girl in her mind. Because Georgia was carrying the embryo that might have been Belle's third child had she carried, she assumed it was a girl all along. She was desperate to find out, and a little disappointed that Georgia wasn't going to find out. "I think it's a girl," Belle said. "I couldn't bear to wait. Tash wanted to wait with Cora, but I was insistent, and then we found out for Ada too."

Georgia was silent for a moment, and then spoke. "The hardest part of not knowing is coming up with two names."

"Oh, I had two names anyway. I love knowing that if I were a boy, I would have been Angus, and if Alex were a boy, she would have been…well…Alex. Alexander, not Alexandra, obviously. So, I wanted my kids to have that. I told Tash we had to come up with names before we found out the sex."

"How did you come up with Cora and Ada? They're lovely names."

"Thanks. When we lived in the UK, I worked with a wonderful Irish girl called Cora, and I always liked her name. When I was pregnant, I suggested Cora if it was a girl, and maybe Caleb if she was a boy."

"Caleb is nice too."

"Yes, I think I like the hard c sound, because I picked Corey if Ada was a boy. But Tash was worried about Cora and Corey being so similar." Georgia grimaced, clearly showing she agreed with Tash.

"I hadn't even thought about it. I should have, because, well, Annabelle and Alexandra." She shrugged as she referred to her and her sister's names. "It always seemed a bit much. That's why we use our nicknames, I think."

Georgia laughed. "Annabelle and Alexandra are much better, but Cora and Corey are a bit much."

"Yeah, they really are. She picked Noah."

"I like Noah. How did you pick Ada?"

"It wasn't after anyone we knew or anything. Tash found it in a baby name book, and I really liked it. Short, but a pretty name, and it seemed to go with Cora. Nothing over the top, but pleasant. I'm so happy with both of their names."

"I like them too. It's so hard to decide. I want something that goes well with Reid, but I like a few one syllable names. Jade Reid, Blake Reid, Claire Reid, James Reid—I don't think any of them sound good."

"You've got a bit of time to decide. Keep thinking it over. I wrote a list, and then spent a week talking to the baby using that name and realising it wouldn't work for me. Because even once we knew the sex, we weren't 100 per cent locked in on the baby's name, we kept going back and forth."

"That's a good idea, actually."

*

AT THE HOSPITAL the next morning, they were sitting in the waiting room with Jo, catching up on the week they'd had. "I have a lot to share," Georgia laughed, "from the movies to the TV shows, and the books—it has been an eventful week for me!"

"Sounds perfect, actually," Jo mused.

"I do joke, but I actually had a great week. And Belle has looked after me so well. I'm very lucky." Belle smiled at Georgia.

Jo glanced at her watch. "This wait is taking forever. My tummy's rumbling. Anyone want to share some hot chips?"

Georgia's eyes widened in anticipation. "Make it a large. I'm eating for two, remember!"

Jo jumped up and started to walk away. "Belle?"

"I wouldn't say no to pinching a couple, put it that way."

"I bet she comes back with a coffee too. The chips are just a ruse to hide her coffee addiction." Georgia laughed as Jo sailed down the hallway.

"Oh, if she was offering coffee and chips, she might have become my favourite person!"

Georgia feigned disgust. "And there I was thinking I was your favourite person."

Belle felt the moment turn awkward.

"I'm starving. I'm so looking forward to chips, actually." Georgia broke the silence.

"I mustn't have been feeding you enough...since you're eating for two."

"I actually have eaten so much, thank you. You have given me loads of comfort food. I think my tummy has grown this week." Georgia stood up and held her hands under her bump. Belle was grinning at it as Georgia paraded back and forth. At that moment, two women walked down the hall, past the open waiting room, then one instantly did a double-take and returned. "Georgia?"

Belle and Georgia looked up, and Belle cringed when she noticed it was Emily whose bump was getting much larger.

"Tash!" Emily called down the hall. "It's Belle and Georgia."

Georgia was still embracing her bump when Tash looked at her and then to Belle. "What are you doing here?" she asked in confusion.

"I'm having a scan," Georgia said. "Did Belle tell you I'm having a baby too?"

"No." Tash said. "Congratulations. How far along are you?"

"Nearly seventeen weeks," Georgia said proudly. "Actually, I found out the day of the fashion gala, when I met you. When I found out about your pregnancy"—she directed that at Emily—"but it was too early for me to share. I thought Belle might have told you." Belle sat there awkwardly, and she noticed Tash shoot a strange look in her direction.

"Well, no, she didn't, but she doesn't always tell me

about her friend's pregnancies." Belle wondered if she imagined it, but she thought she picked up an edge to Tash's voice and wondered what on earth Tash was thinking. "It's nice that you're such close friends that you can be Georgia's support person at the scan, Belle." Okay, she hadn't imagined it, Belle thought, the edge to her voice was clearly there.

At that moment, Jo burst into the waiting room, carrying three overflowing bags of hot chips, and balancing a coffee in her elbow. "The queue was so long that by the time I got to the top, I *had* to get a coffee. I would have texted you, but"—she shrugged—"my hands were full. Hi, I'm Jo." Jo grinned when she saw Tash and Emily standing over Belle and Georgia. Noticing Emily's bump, Jo said, "Sit down, please, you can have some chips. I bought heaps. I can feed an army of pregnant women."

"Oh, no," Tash protested, "we have to rush."

Emily shook her head. "We don't. We don't have anywhere to be." Tash shot her a look that Belle remembered from their days together as being the "shut up, be a team here" signal. She couldn't hide her small grin as she noticed

Emily ignore the look—either she hadn't noticed or was deliberately avoiding it, a skill that Belle herself had tried to master over the years. Emily sat down next to Georgia and said, "I'm starving, and those chips look great."

Tash practically rolled her eyes in front of them, but only Belle noticed, as Georgia and Emily shared chips and pregnancy stories, and Jo watched on their chatter, participating when she could. Tash finally, and reluctantly, sat down next to Belle. "What's going on?" Tash asked.

"We're just waiting for this scan. We'll be called in soon, I think." Belle wasn't giving anything anyway. She needed to tell Tash the story, but now wasn't the time or place. Besides, she figured they'd be called in for their appointment soon enough. They'd been waiting long enough after all.

"Three of you here? They usually only let one support person in for a scan, don't they?" Belle glanced at Georgia. On the plus side, catching up with Tash and Emily seemed to have reduced Georgia's fears; she was now looking quite relaxed and flushed in the cheeks as Georgia and Emily shared all their aches, pains, and pregnancy laughs and horror stories. There was something about pregnancy that seemed to unite women. Tash was clearly confused, or fishing for information, and Belle was trying to work out what Tash was thinking. She liked that, for a change, Tash was the one left guessing.

Belle merely shrugged in response. "I'm not sure—we just both wanted to be here today. We will see when they call Georgia in. Did you have a scan too? How is every-thing?"

"We had an appointment with the midwife." Tash pointed toward the antenatal rooms. "She said everything is going really well. Emily's twenty-five weeks now. Not too long, though the last trimester feels the longest, from memory."

"How are the girls?" Belle asked.

"Doing well. Cora has soccer this afternoon."

"Oh, of course. Who is going to soccer?" Belle asked casually, as if she was just making conversation.

"Just me—Emily will stay home with Ada. We had a couple of busy days, so it'll be good for Ada to have a quiet one in with Em."

"Is it okay if I pop along to watch Cora? We could have a chat?" Belle was hoping to have an opportunity to talk to Tash, and clearly from the way Tash was looking at her, seeking answers, it seemed important.

"That would be *great,*" Tash said pointedly. "Five thirty p.m. at the Griffith ovals. I'm sure Cora would love to see you there."

The scan, thankfully, went well, and both Belle and Jo were allowed in the room as support people. Although the doctor indicated that the placenta was still in a concerning position, she was confident it would move by the birth. If it didn't, Georgia would need a C-section. Georgia asked her about work and bed rest. The doctor shook her head. "You don't need bed rest. You can work but try to take it easy when you're home. Don't carry anything too heavy and avoid sex. We'll see how things are again at the twenty-week scan."

After the doctor left the room, Georgia turned to Jo and laughed. "No sex, dammit! Not like there was any on the agenda."

The three women went to lunch after the scan. "So,

what's the plan now? You're back at work next week?" Jo asked. "Or will you take some more time off?"

"No. All back to normal next week. I want to save up my leave as much as I can."

Jo agreed. "That makes sense."

"I'm still a little anxious, but I'll just need to take it easy. At least Belle will get her spare room back."

Belle was disappointed to hear it. "You don't need to go. I'm happy for you to stay with me until the twenty-week scan. I know eventually you'll want to be back at home to 'nest,' but I've got heaps of room, and I think it's been working. If you want."

"It's been working because you've been feeding me loads of carbs and sweet treats." Georgia's eyes were sparkling. "I don't mind. I'm okay at home."

"But you do need to do groceries, cook, clean, do laundry at home…" Jo said. "You being with Belle makes me worry less, I must admit. It's probably selfish of me to say that."

Georgia looked at Belle, and Belle smiled. "It's up to you, George."

"Well, I'll stay until the end of the weekend, at least. That was always our plan. But I may as well stay. It's nice to have the company."

"Just in case there's any more bleeding." Jo said, and Georgia nodded.

"Oh, the girls are back tomorrow, aren't they? Are you sure it's okay for me to stay?" Georgia spoke once she realised.

"Sure. I'll chat to Tash this afternoon. I've told Tash I will go watch Cora play soccer."

"That was a bit weird seeing her," Georgia admitted. "Of all the people to see at the hospital."

"Well, you and Emily are both pregnant. The antenatal clinic is where pregnant women go," Belle said, but she was certainly sounding more casual than she felt. It had been the worst timing.

Georgia nodded her agreement.

"Who are they?" Jo asked. "I meant to ask before, and then we got called in for the scan, and then got carried away with all of that."

"The tall one is Belle's ex-wife," Georgia explained, "of

twenty years." She raised her eyebrows as she spoke.

"Gosh, you don't look old enough to have been married twenty years," Jo said.

"We weren't actually married and we started dating when I was fifteen."

"Oh, childhood sweethearts. So cute."

"Yes, so cute until she cheated on me." Belle could hear the bitterness in her voice and hated that Tash still made her resort to that.

"So she's the other mother to your kids? Did you carry or did she?"

"I carried, but yes, she's the other mother. And Emily is her new partner—not the one she cheated on me with, thank goodness—and they're having a baby."

"Using the same sperm donor as the donor for this one," Georgia said, pointing to her stomach.

It all pieced together for Jo, and she sighed. "Complicated, isn't it?"

*

CORA WAS THRILLED to see both of her mothers at soccer,

but neither of them actually paid much attention to the game.

"So, what made you take the morning off work, and go to the hospital with Georgia? What's going on there?" Tash's question was pointed, and Belle had no idea what she was thinking.

"Georgia and I met through Alex some time ago. We've become really close friends. She had an issue with her pregnancy, and I wanted to be there to help her."

"Okay, but that's it?" Belle didn't answer her immediately, and Tash didn't wait for a response, she kept talking. "I mean, you don't owe me an explanation, but it was a bit strange. She had another friend there."

"Her cousin," Belle interrupted.

"Right. So, are you dating?"

Belle didn't know whether to just tell her, and what to say, so just shook her head in response.

"But you're interested in her?"

"Tash, she's carrying one of our embryos."

Tash's eyebrows shot up and she reeled backwards. "I beg your pardon?"

"She's carrying one of the embryos. We weren't going to use them."

"Wow. So, she is your girlfriend, or a friend you donated to?"

"I donated to her," Belle confessed.

"Right. And you made that decision on your own?" It was very clear that Tash was annoyed.

"I wouldn't have, but you told me the embryos were mine to do what I wanted with them. You didn't want any responsibilities over them. I probably should have asked you, though."

"Damn right you should have asked me. I even told you that Emily and I were considering it, and we're in a relationship. And not using our embryos." Tash stepped away from her. Belle felt awful, watching Tash pacing, clearly upset. She then returned. "So now Cora, Ada, my new baby, and Georgia's baby are all going to be related?"

"Biologically." Belle nodded. "But you wanted to use the same donor as the girls knowing there were embryos out there."

"Embryos I thought *you* might use or discard. I didn't

think you'd be giving them to a stranger."

"Except, as I said, she's become one of my closest friends."

Tash softened and looked at Belle in the eyes. "I thought you had a crush on her, at the gala. That's why I said you should go home in her car." A moment of realisation crossed Tash's face. "Oh, that's why she drove that night." She paused, then added, "But I could see something between you. And even today." She narrowed her eyes and looked closely at Belle. "I was really happy for you, but also a little...jealous to see you so happy. But if she made you happy, I wanted to help, so I suggested you go home with her. I wasn't sure, but there was something there."

Belle shot Tash a confused look. "How can you say that? That you were a little jealous? What right do *you* have to be jealous, Tash?" It was now Belle's chance to ask a pointed question. "Seriously? I loved you so much, I gave you everything. I built my entire life around you! And you threw that in my face, but now *you're* jealous because I have a...a friend?"

"A friend you got pregnant! Anyway, it seemed like a

crush to me, or more than that. Did you donate the embryo to her because you want a relationship with her?"

"No, I wasn't that close with her then. It's grown." Suddenly she felt bashful.

"But you are interested in her? I've seen the way you look at her." Tash paused, and then spoke up, "It was how you used to look at me."

"Who cares what it is? I'm a free agent." Belle couldn't believe Tash even thought she had a right to have an opinion, and though she was annoyed, she was also secretly pleased that it bothered Tash.

"I suppose you're right. Is she interested in you?"

"She's straight."

"Oh." Tash exhaled. "Oh, Belle. I just don't want to see you get hurt and this...this..."

Belle didn't want her pity, so just continued, "Anyway, Georgia has stayed with me this past week. Her pregnancy is challenging, and so I had her stay, just so she had some company in case anything happened. I was wondering if you'd mind if she stayed when I had the girls. Like this weekend?"

"I don't know her very well," Tash responded. Belle shot her another look—a look that called Tash out as a hypocrite, and thankfully Tash knew her well enough to read it. She hurriedly added, "I trust your judgement though. And I am happy for her and hope it all goes well."

"Thank you, I appreciate that. I'd hate for something to happen to her when she's alone."

"For her sake or the baby's?"

That was the million-dollar question, wasn't it?

*

"HOW DID IT go?" Georgia asked when Belle returned. She was standing up in the kitchen making dinner, and Belle noticed she was really glowing, radiating happiness and beauty.

"As I expected it would. She's annoyed, but not with you. Just that I didn't talk to her about it all before I offered. And I should have." Belle did feel bad about that. "It just wasn't on my mind because she'd made this big song and dance about how the embryos were mine to make all the decisions about." Belle looked more intently at Georgia.

"You're looking really good. What are you doing in the kitchen?"

"I'm feeling good, and so I wanted to make you dinner. I think I felt relieved that the scan went well, and I just wanted to make dinner to thank you for everything you've done for me. It's nothing special. Burritos."

"Well, it smells amazing."

During dinner, they talked non-stop about everything and anything, which Belle found particularly noteworthy given they'd barely been apart. One topic Belle did not want to discuss was the situation with Tash, but Georgia raised it.

"So, Tash is okay that I'm staying here when the girls are here? Because, if she's not, I'm feeling good, and I know I'll be fine on my own."

"Actually you being here was the least of her worries. She's fine."

"So, she's worried about the baby?" Georgia's hands instinctively went to her stomach.

"No, it was more that I hadn't talked to her, but she also seems to understand why. She's cool. She's happy for you."

*

THE NEXT AFTERNOON, Belle raced from work to day care and after-school care to pick up the girls, and then took them home. Georgia was sitting at the dining table doing a thousand-piece jigsaw puzzle Belle had encouraged her to start.

Belle lent down beside her daughters and spoke calmly, "Cora, Ada, this is my friend Georgia. She's the one I was telling you about."

"Hi, Georgia," said Cora, and Ada smiled.

"Hello, wow, I love your dress, Ada. And, Cora, I love the bows in your hair." Belle smiled at the interaction as Georgia continued. "I'm just doing a jigsaw, but these pieces are super tiny. I thought I'd pack it away and get you to help me with another one I tried to do today while you were at school. I couldn't get it done." Georgia packed the puzzle away in a jigsaw storage bag that meant she could continue where she left off later, and then got a box of children's puzzles out. She sat on the ground with the children and asked for their help in piecing together the puzzle. The girls instantly became comfortable with her, and Belle's heart warmed at the sight.

After lots of games, then bath time and dinner time, the girls were finally in bed. Georgia let out a sigh. "You have two great girls. You and Tash have done a great job with them."

"Thank you. We're pretty proud of them. It hasn't been easy, the fifty-fifty, I'll be honest, but Tash and I are in a good place now. I wonder how the new baby will change things for Tash."

Georgia thought for a moment. "Babies change everything. I'm petrified. I feel like I spent so long working toward getting pregnant, I never actually stopped and thought about parenting. Pregnancy was the goal for me. Obviously, I know pregnancy leads to parenting, but it was such a far-off dream, I never really gave it much thought. And here I am"—she rubbed her belly—"wondering how everything will be. Wondering if I'll do a good job."

"From where I'm sitting, I think you'll be an amazing mum. You were beautiful with the girls just then."

Georgia blushed as she spoke. "Thank you. I'm flattered. You must remember I'm a grade one teacher, so I have a bit of practice with kids of this age. The jigsaw puzzle is one of my favourite tricks to get the kids comfortable with me." Belle had forgotten Georgia's job as she'd watched the exchange between her and the girls—all she'd seen with someone with enough patience and interest to be an amazing mother. Georgia continued, "So the question is, how will I handle my child when they're pushing back? A difficult teenager? A toddler having a tantrum? An argumentative ten-year-old? It will be a challenge!"

"That's parenting for you, but it's also very rewarding I think you'll be perfect, and most of all, it took you a long time to get here. You want it."

"I do." Tears appeared in Georgia's eyes, as she was pensive. "I'm so excited. I'm scared, but I'm excited. And meeting your girls made it so much more real for me. They're so adorable. If this baby is half as cute as them, I'll be half-way there."

*

THE WEEKEND FLEW by with home movies, long walks, plenty of jigsaw puzzles, games, and a lot of baking. Once the weekend was over, Georgia agreed with Belle that she was happy to stay a little longer. Belle and Georgia got into a routine with the girls. Georgia went back to work, and Belle was back in the office full time, so Belle would pick them up from day care and after-school care, and Georgia would be home, making an early start on getting dinner ready. Belle looked forward to the afternoons more than she ever had. Seeing Georgia in the kitchen as she and the girls bustled in made her heart sing. Georgia had made herself at home and often had music playing on the stereo as she cooked. Her hair would sway as she'd sing along, unashamedly. Sometimes Belle would arrive home and sense that they were the family she'd always dreamt of for her and the girls. All Belle wanted to do when she arrived home was embrace her, kiss her, and be together. Then she'd remind herself that the woman happily singing in her kitchen was just her friend…her very straight friend…her very straight and pregnant friend.

Chapter Eighteen

AT THE END of the week, Cora and Ada would return to Tash and Emily, and in anticipation, Belle and Georgia discussed plans for the weekend. They decided to invite Nikki and Jo over to hang out on the Friday night and agreed they would go to the markets on the Sunday morning. Other than that, they planned a quiet weekend in. Georgia was still wanting to take it easy, especially with her busy week of teaching.

*

JO AND NIKKI got on like a house on fire, just like Belle had expected. Belle had quickly realised she loved the comfortable ease Jo brought to any catch up. Conversations were light, flowed easily, and yet were not necessarily shallow. It was also nice for Nikki and Georgia to spend more time together, as Belle was always talking to one about the other. After a few drinks, Nikki suggested they play a board game, but Jo rolled her eyes and said it was more fun to chat. "I bring out the board games when I'm struggling to find something to talk about. I don't think we need one."

"I don't think you'd ever struggle to find something to talk about," Belle laughed.

Georgia smiled as she spoke. "Absolutely not. When we were growing up, we could always count on Jo being the one to come up with new ideas, or conversation starters. She made us play truth and dare all the time, or run around the neighbourhood toilet papering cars, or—"

"You toilet papered cars?" Belle raised an eyebrow. "Gee, you're naughtier than I thought." Belle had a twinkle in her eye as she teased Georgia. "I always thought you were a good girl."

"I'm a good girl, but my cousin is a bad influence on me. She made me do it."

"Hmm, I don't know if that's a defence in a court of law," Belle mused aloud.

Jo had rushed off to the kitchen while they were talking about their childhood. She entered the lounge with a large dip platter, crisps, and a platter of brownies that she had brought with her. "I did cater," Belle said, gesturing to the platter of cheese and dips she had out, "but I always welcome extra food."

"I know you did, but I never come empty-handed. I like extra snacks. And Georgia is eating for two, after all. We have to support her through this." Everyone agreed and piled crackers high with dips as they chatted.

At the end of the evening, Jo thanked Belle. "This was just what I needed," she said.

"Me too," Belle enthused. "It's so nice that we all get along so well."

"Exactly." Belle liked that Jo had somehow fitted in so neatly into her own life. While she was obviously much closer to both Nikki and Georgia, she'd thoroughly enjoyed

Jo's company and genuinely looked forward to the next time they'd all be together again.

*

ON SUNDAY MORNING, Belle and Georgia headed out to the local markets. They strolled side by side at the markets, picking up items, laughing at some crazy finds, and sampling every food item they could find from breads to dips, and, of course, fudge and cakes. They finished up eating pides and drinking smoothies, while chatting about the week ahead, Georgia's maternity leave plans, her hopes and dreams for her baby. Their hearts and bellies full, they strolled to the car and returned home, where they had quiet afternoons pottering around. Belle did her washing for the week, while Georgia spent some time reading.

Later in the afternoon, Georgia rugged up and called out to Belle, "Are you okay if I use the kitchen?" Georgia had bought bags of produce at the markets, so Belle wondered what she might be making.

"Georgia. You don't even have to ask," Belle responded from the laundry. She smiled—although she enjoyed living alone, she had gotten used to the company, and wondered what Georgia's plans would be after the twenty-week scan. If all was going well, she expected that Georgia would move home, ready to prepare for the birth of her baby. If things weren't looking good, she wondered if she might continue staying at her house. She thought Georgia might be worried that she would overstay her welcome by the time the twenty-week scan rolled around. Belle really wanted to make sure she felt comfortable. She knew that once the baby's arrival was imminent, Georgia would have to head home, but she wasn't ready to have Georgia leave just yet. She wouldn't like a housemate long-term, but being around Georgia really made her happy and comfortable in a way she hadn't felt in many years.

Georgia produced a thick, creamy vegetable and lentil soup with crunchy bread for dinner. "I found the lentils in the bottom of the pantry."

Belle grimaced. "I wonder how long they've been there."

"That's the beauty of lentils. It doesn't really matter. And I'm pleased you obviously didn't care about them. I thought I might be rushing to the store this evening to buy you a replacement packet."

"I honestly can't even remember how they got there in the first place. But seriously, you should make yourself at home. What's mine is yours."

Georgia joked, "Those sapphire earrings you're wearing? Hand them over. What's yours is mine." The twinkle in her eyes told Belle she was joking, even if her tone was deadpan.

Belle's hands instinctively went to her ears, and she grinned. "These were a gift from my parents for my thirtieth birthday. They're simple but pretty. I really like them," Belle explained.

Georgia nodded. "I love sapphires. They're so beautiful. I'd noticed your earrings before, so y'know, now everything is mine…" She trailed off, grinning.

"No, but seriously, I mean, you don't have to panic if you finish a jar of jam or whatever."

"Mmm," Georgia responded. "I've been here a while though. At first it was because I was a 'patient,' but now I'm back at work and doing well. I suppose I should be thinking about returning home." Belle's fear was being realised.

"You are doing well, but we don't want to risk any-thing." Belle frowned. "Look, I'm not trying to keep you here if you don't want to be, but please know that you're welcome here. At least until the twenty-week scan, but I'm even happy if you're here until the birth. Then you and the baby can settle in at your home." Even as Belle spoke, she was concerned about why she wanted her around so much. Her mother and Tash were both worried she was going to get hurt, and if she was really honest, Belle could under stand why.

"Well, let's keep the plan to stay until the scan. Then we can decide. I like the company too."

*

LATER THAT EVENING, Belle was sitting on the couch watching a TV show when Georgia emerged from the bath-room in a fluffy pink towel wrapped around her body. The towel was pulled tight over her growing stomach and swol-len breasts. Her arms and legs were tanned, and her long hair hung down, wet over her shoulders. Georgia said, "I meant to say you should just watch that movie—I forgot I had some work to do tonight. I'll bring my laptop out and sit with you. Once I'm dressed, that is."

Belle couldn't help but stare at the beauty in front of her. Georgia looked incredible, but Belle knew she was staring too much. She tried to look away, but instead she just nodded, feeling incredibly turned on. Georgia had no clue the effect she was having on Belle. "Okay, I can wait for you."

"Don't wait for me," Georgia said. Belle realised she was talking about the movie but wondered if she was just imagining an undertone.

Chapter Nineteen

SHE HAD IT bad for Georgia, she realised. In bed that evening, Belle thought about ways to protect her heart without shutting Georgia out of her life. She knew how much she wanted Georgia to stay as her housemate to ensure she was looked after during the pregnancy, but she'd now realised that wasn't the only reason she loved having Georgia around. She wanted to maintain the friendship she was quickly building with Georgia, and she loved her company, so didn't want to put a stop to their arrangement, despite falling hard.

Maybe she needed a distraction so that she didn't get hurt. Contacting Riley sprang to mind. They'd had an enjoyable evening, and it had taken her mind off things. Perhaps it would help with Belle's raging libido that was firing up around Georgia. Riley was never going to be the love of her life but maybe a bit of fun wouldn't go astray. Other than her evening with Riley a few weeks back, it had been quite some time. Getting a bit of action would no doubt distract her. Belle wondered if this was a crazy idea, or a genius idea.

She quickly arranged to meet Riley in a bar one evening after work. Riley jumped at the chance to catch up, no doubt hoping to continue where they'd left off last time. They greeted each other with a chaste kiss on the cheek and chatted over a drink.

"I was really pleased to get your text message," Riley said. "I wondered if that meant you changed your mind."

"I still don't want a relationship. I was thinking more about stress relief." Belle laughed shyly. "Or just company."

"Your wish is my command. I'm definitely happy to offer that." Riley reached out to hold Belle's hand. The conversation flowed easily, though Riley ensured it was loaded with innuendo. Belle was clear where she stood with Riley and what Riley was looking for. She was easy company, and though she wasn't Georgia, she would help to get Belle's mind off Georgia.

Finally Riley asked, "How's your friend? And the baby?"

"Georgia. She's doing well. Baby's still cooking okay. Actually, Georgia's come to stay at my house for a bit; she lives alone."

"Ah, okay. So she's a single mum? I did wonder why she called you in the middle of the night. That makes sense."

"Yes, she's a single mum." Belle couldn't help but think this wasn't helping her get Georgia off her mind.

"That must be hard, to be single during pregnancy. Probably not what she was wanting." Riley sighed, probably assuming Georgia had broken up with the father of her baby.

"She conceived single, actually. Solo mum by choice." Belle wasn't sure that Georgia would call herself a solo mum by choice, but it seemed the easiest way to explain that it hadn't been unplanned. Of course, Georgia would have preferred to be in a relationship, but she wanted a baby more than she'd wanted to wait and risk not finding someone.

"Oh, that's really cool. And it's really nice she can rely on you."

Riley was right—it was nice that Georgia had her support. Georgia was sitting home alone while Belle was flirting with a possible 'friend with benefits.' Belle sighed and finally spoke up. "You know, I've been thinking. The time might not be right for me right now. I enjoyed everything we had, and maybe one day in the future... I'm so sorry to get you here. I really thought I would go for it, but now I realise it's not the right time for me. Between my friend, and other things. I'm so sorry." And with that, Belle picked up her things and made her way home. There would be other times for flirting, for now she needed to be home, with Georgia, providing that support. Sure, she had a little crush. She could move on from that.

*

"ARE YOU DOING anything much today?" Belle asked Georgia the following Sunday morning.

Georgia put down her book and yawned. "No, you?"

"I'm taking the girls for a roast lunch at Mum and Dad's. Would you like to come with us?"

Georgia responded instantly. "Sounds lovely, but I don't want to intrude."

"Nonsense. Alex will be there—I'm sure she'd love to see you. The kids would love you there, and Mum and Dad believe the more the merrier."

"Okay, but can we stop for a box of chocolates on the way?"

After the chocolates were purchased, they arrived at Belle's parents' house, and the children jumped out of the car, with Belle and Georgia following closely behind.

"Grandma!" Ada went running in to the house, embracing Julie and then Clive as if she hadn't seen them in a year, rather than a couple of weeks. Belle watched on, bemused. Julie and Clive then greeted Cora before finally focusing their attention on Georgia. She apologised for intruding on such a nice family get-together.

"Don't be silly, love," Julie said. "The more the merrier for Sunday roasts. I've even made Yorkshire puddings."

"Yes!" Alex fist pumped the air in mock excitement.

Georgia handed over the chocolates to Julie. "A thank you for hosting me."

"Oh, lovely. You didn't really need to do that, darling, but I'll certainly enjoy them watching the telly tonight. I'll just have to make sure Clive doesn't get any."

The mood was light during the family catch up. Julie served up large platters of food on the kitchen bench and encouraged everyone to pile their plates high, and they did just that. "Remember you're eating for two," Belle said to Georgia, as she was a little more restrained filling her plate compared to the rest of them. "Don't be shy."

Georgia put a few more pieces of potatoes, pumpkin, and sweet potatoes on her plate. "I love pumpkin," she said.

"I love sweet potatoes, Georgia," Cora said. "They look like pumpkins, but they're tastier." Everyone laughed.

During lunch, Alex shared that she was going to go on a trip to New Zealand. "Just the two weeks during the school holidays," she said. "It'll be nice to get away from it all."

"Ah, lovely. Who are you going to go with, love? Another teacher? Or is this a solo trip?" her mother asked. Alex had done a few solo trips, but they were usually to resorts in Queensland rather than overseas. Still, New Zealand wasn't exactly far away, but Belle suspected Alex would be travelling around.

"Oh, Anton. He's going to take a few weeks off," Alex said, smiling. The people around the table exchanged glances. Belle really didn't think that there was anything happening between Alex and Anton, but she thought that Alex and Anton themselves were the last people to know that they had something between them.

After everyone had nearly finished their full plates, Belle asked, "Did you do anything for dessert?" Dessert was never a guarantee with Julie's lunches—sometimes she lavished desserts on them, and other times she would say, "Oh, you don't need dessert with lunch."

Generally, if her granddaughters were there, she was a little more likely to offer up dessert, but even that didn't mean it was automatic. Belle was hopeful. It sounded crazy, but there was something about stuffing yourself full with a big lunch and then finishing it up with a chocolate pudding or cake, or whatever. Thankfully they were in luck, and her mum produced two desserts—a raspberry torte and a chocolate cake. The children were allowed to pick their dessert first and took large slices of chocolate cake. When it was finally her turn, Belle did the same.

Georgia took a slice of the raspberry torte. "This is amazing," she said to Julie. "Thank you, this whole lunch has been beautiful. I do love a hot roast, especially on a cold Sunday afternoon."

"Oh, me too," Julie said. "It brings back memories of my childhood, and so I've always done it since Clive and I married. All through Belle and Alexandra's childhoods. These days the girls don't always turn up, but usually if Belle has the girls, she'll try to get here. Have you been thinking about what rituals you might like to do when you have the baby? Or are you a fly-by-the-seat-of-your-pants person?"

"I haven't given it much thought, but I'll spoil the baby rotten every Christmas. I don't know what rituals I'll do, though. Whether I'll do a weekly roast or anything. All I know is family is very important to me. My cousin has regular catch ups, and I visit my mum a bit. If you're keen, I'd love for the baby to get to know you all, too, but I understand if you'd rather not."

Julie and Clive grinned. "Oh, darling, we'd love that. Completely up to you, but we'd definitely love that. It's your baby, we understand, but the way we see it, you're family. Right, Clive?"

"Absolutely. We always say anyone is part of the family, but given the circumstances"—he gestured to her stomach—"you're definitely family to us." Belle hoped that Georgia didn't feel awkward about her parents carrying on, but it seemed to be quite the opposite—she seemed delighted to be so easily welcomed into the fold.

"How long are you taking off work?" Alex asked, maintaining the attention on Georgia and her pregnancy.

"The baby is due in December. Ideally, I'll take off all of next year. I can then start the school year the following January, after the baby is already one. Being a single mum will be a juggle."

"That's actually good timing," Alex said. "If you wanted to return a little earlier, you could always do some relief teaching. Some part time stuff if your money doesn't quite stretch far enough."

"That's not a bad idea," Belle said to Georgia. "It could give the baby the day care experience a day or two here or there before it's in full time."

Georgia agreed. "It's something to keep in mind. For now, my mind is on getting through the rest of this pregnancy." She rubbed her stomach affectionately.

"How's it going?" Julie asked.

"I don't know if Belle has told you—it's been a little difficult. Placenta is in the wrong position. If it doesn't move, I might need a C-section, but otherwise everything is good. I had some rest for a while, but they don't really recommend bed rest or anything like that these days. It's a wait-and-see thing, and while I'm not so keen to have a C-section, I know it's no big deal."

"Oh, it's not. Millions of women have them. Gosh, it's a very basic procedure these days." Julie spoke with authority, despite not having had a C-section herself. "What matters is the love you give the child, not the way they got here." Belle wondered if she meant the birth, or the donated embryo, or both.

*

"I LOVE YOUR family," Georgia said. "Your mum and dad seemed lovely at the gala, and of course I think you and Alex are great. I was still nervous, though, but I shouldn't have been. The moment I walked in, I felt very welcome."

"Grandad is very funny," Ada spoke up from the backseat of the car.

"He is funny," Georgia agreed. Clive usually cracked constant silly dad jokes. Today he was thankfully a little more restrained, but still cracked a few.

"And Grandma looks after us," Cora said. Belle always felt fortunate that her parents helped out as much as they needed with the girls.

"That's true," Belle said to Georgia. "I'm lucky—Mum always helps out, but even if Tash needs some help, Mum will do it. And Tash's parents, for that matter. We're very lucky that way, and neither of them worry about whose 'week' it is or anything. I suppose that's the one advantage after breaking up after such a long time. Our families knew us well—since childhood."

"Oh, I get the sense that your family would help out, even if you'd dated Tash five minutes."

"That's probably true," Belle mused aloud. "They're just that kind of family."

Georgia agreed. "I can tell."

"Do you have much family support?"

Georgia had told Belle that she was close to her family, and she knew that she'd confided in her mum about the embryo donation, so Belle assumed that Georgia did.

"Yes, Mum will be amazing, I think. I'm her only child, and this is probably her only grandchild. She's thrilled. The biggest issue will be getting her to give us some space. I'd love you to meet Mum, actually. But our relationship is different; it's just the two of us. Dad died when I was twelve, and Mum and I have a very quiet relationship. It's not a bustling family like yours. It's just the two of us sitting looking at one another. I suppose that will change when the baby's here, but I think it might feel a bit intense for you. She's so close to my Aunty Susan. That's Jo's mum. When Dad died, we moved in with Aunty Susan, her husband Lance, and Jo and Sarah. We lived with them for about ten months, maybe longer, I can't remember. Mum wouldn't have made it without them, and I think that's why I'm so close to Jo. Sarah, too, but Jo's really been my rock growing up. Actually, maybe we could have a catch up at Jo's house. Bring the girls along. Sarah has kids too. You could meet Mum in a more relaxed environment that way."

"I'd love that."

The next two weeks were a blur—Belle was particularly busy at work, but Belle and Georgia had developed a good routine of living together and just having fun. The twenty-week scan went well, though there was some minor movement of the placenta. The doctors wanted to check her over again a month later. By the weekend, Belle and Georgia were looking forward to their time with Cora and Ada. On Saturday afternoon, the four of them headed to Jo's house with the intention of Belle and the girls meeting more of Georgia's family including Georgia's mum.

"Hi, Mum." Georgia embraced a short, plump woman

with salt-and-pepper hair. "Belle"—Georgia reached out to bring Belle closer—"this is my mum, Mary. Mum, this is my friend, Belle."

"Hi, Mary," Belle said shyly.

Mary hugged Belle and kissed her on the cheek. "Hello," she said, "it's lovely to finally meet you after so long." Quickly the introductions kept coming—Georgia's Aunty Susan, Uncle Lance, and Cousin Susan, her husband Matthew, and three children aged between five and eight. Jo, of course, made Belle feel really comfortable, and the food smelt amazing. "I've got three different lasagnes and plenty of garlic bread and pizza in the oven. It's a carb fest here today," she said, laughing.

"Three different lasagnes?"

"Beef, vegetarian, and chicken." Jo shrugged. "I cater for variety."

"I brought salads," Mary said to Belle. "I hope you like couscous; I've tried a new one. But I also brought pasta salad, and a green salad if you don't."

"They all sound fabulous. I can't wait. Georgia and I brought brownies." Georgia had told her that everyone brought something along to these get-togethers—they were so frequent—but that offerings could be anything as basic as a nice bottle of wine, or a new cheese. Usually the guests would let Jo know what they were bringing, but Jo had told Georgia not to worry—she was pregnant, after all, and Belle was the guest. Belle said she couldn't come empty-handed, so the four of them had spent the morning messing up the kitchen making various brownies—some with white chocolate chips, some with nuts, some with icing and some just very fudgy.

"I also brought dessert today," Susan said. "My world-famous cheesecakes."

"World-famous," Jo scoffed, toward Belle. "I mean, they're very good—and they certainly feature a lot in our get-togethers, but no one outside of here"—she gestured in a circular motion around the family—"knows about these cheesecakes. Oprah Winfrey is hardly promoting them, y'know." Everyone laughed, and Belle felt very comfortable in their presence.

Just before the food was served, Belle realised she hadn't seen her children in a long time. "I'll go find them,"

Georgia said and apparently found them all in the back-yard, playing together like they'd known one another for years. The eldest of Sarah's children was creating games for the children to play, and they were all participating. They all groaned when they were called in for lunch, but then ate like there was no tomorrow.

"Your family are great," Belle quietly said to Georgia when they had a brief moment alone.

Georgia grinned. "Happy that the baby will have a good extended family?" She rubbed her tummy as she spoke.

Belle smiled wider and nodded. "Yes. I think a support-ive family is so great for kids, and your baby is going to be doted on."

Georgia agreed. "I feel very lucky, and I'm pleased you approve."

Chapter Twenty

THE FOLLOWING WEEK, Belle asked Tash if she could catch up with her. Tash readily agreed and asked Emily to look after the girls, so they were alone. They caught up at a small coffee shop mid-way between their houses that they'd used in the very early days for child-handover. Wondering how she could ever move on and trust another relationship had been on her mind ever since they broke up, but somehow, living with Georgia made her question things more. She didn't know how she was going to tackle the questions she needed the answers to, but she felt a desperate urge to find out more. She was already seated when Tash walked into the café.

"Hi, what's up?" Tash asked. "Everything okay?"

"Yes, everything is good."

Tash was clearly relieved, but likely more confused than anything else. They ordered coffee and snacks, then returned to the table. "So this is just a friendly catch up, then?" Tash's eyebrows were raised; she clearly figured Belle had something on her mind.

"I wanted to know why you cheated on me."

Tash instantly shifted uncomfortably in her seat and then asked Belle why. "We've moved past 'us,' haven't we? I thought we were in a good place right now. Why are you worrying about the end of our relationship now?"

Belle agreed. "We are in a good spot. This isn't about you at all. Obviously, it's about finding out why, but it's not about me being in a negative spot about us. It's just… Look, I'm going to be brutally honest here." She had begun to wonder if this was a bad idea.

"Please," Tash urged her.

"We were together since we were kids. Honestly, we

got so close to twenty years. I'd pictured our twentieth an-
niversary. I never questioned my feelings for you. I was so
young, I wasn't planning for the future. I just jumped in.
And trust? I'd have trusted you with my life. But now I'm
thirty-six years old. I've lived. I've loved." She nodded towards Tash. "And I've lost. I'm not that bright-eyed fifteen-
year-old that fell in love with you."

Tash's eyes narrowed as she clearly tried to work out
where this was all going.

Belle continued, "I know our relationship wasn't perfect, but we'd travelled, we had kids, we had plans. We had
dreams to grow old together. And then, suddenly, that
changed. And I'm having trouble… I've not been in another
relationship because I'm scared. I'm scared about putting
my trust in someone. I want to know a bit more. It will help
me to move on."

Tash sighed loudly. "I don't know what I can say. I can
tell you the reasons that we ended, but I don't see how that
will help you to trust someone else. I can't make guarantees,
especially for someone else. All I can say that you shouldn't
protect your heart so much that you end up lonely." Tash

shrugged. "You're a relationship woman. I've been surprised you've been single this long."

"Relationship woman." Belle grimaced. "I don't know what I am. For so long, I was completely devoted to you and the life we planned together. I wonder who I would have been if we hadn't started a relationship so early. I have no idea. Would I have been a relationship woman, or just me? I don't know. But the truth is, I did always have you by my side. I enjoyed that, but I didn't enjoy the aftermath. I don't want that again."

Tash sat back in her chair, looking uncomfortable again. "As I said, I don't know what I can say. You're right; we fell into it. That doesn't mean I didn't adore you—I did—but I got itchy feet. It was all a bit perfect, wasn't it? You were my first kiss, my first relationship. I loved being with you, but I often wondered about the grass on the other side. Didn't you?"

Belle felt just as hurt as she had when they'd ended. Although time had healed things, it still pained her that she hadn't been enough. "No, I didn't. I used to think about ways to make you happier, ways to surprise you, what we'd do next. I used to imagine what we'd be like as grandmothers. I never thought about handing kids over in this café like we used to do. I never thought that that we were going to be moving on with new people. I never thought you'd be having a third child with someone else." She smiled, but knew it was a sad smile. It summed up all the defeat and grief she had felt.

"Okay, well, I never gave all of that much thought. I just wondered. Was I ever the person to settle down with my first love? Wasn't I too wild for that? I thought about dating heaps; I thought about going to nightclubs and dancing the night away. I felt like we'd thrown away our youth by being responsible."

"We weren't that responsible! We ditched our jobs and went overseas. We spent every weekend travelling to new places. We spent all our money and all our time soaking up experiences. I don't know what more you needed to feel alive."

"True, and while that was happening, I didn't give it that much thought. But we came home, bought a five-bedroom house, had babies, and all I could see before me was…nappies, school runs, high school discos, soccer mums… I don't know… It wasn't the life I ever expected for myself."

Belle frowned and bit her lip, but finally spoke. "But you wanted it. And now you'll have all of that with Emily, anyway."

"I know. Silly, really, isn't it?"

Belle sighed loudly. "So why?"

"It's the old story, isn't it? I met Amanda at work, and she was interested in me. She made me feel desired. At home, you were annoyed with me. You never seemed really happy with me anymore. We didn't have much fun. Our relationship felt a bit…transactional, I guess. All the planning, the micro-managing. The girls' schedule, their routine, our needs were last. And I get that, but Amanda was asking me to coffee, or drinks, and we'd catch up, and it was just the two of us. We'd talk and talk, and I felt heard for the first time in a while. When we caught up, it was like we were in a bubble. With you, there was no bubble. We were losing us. We lost what made us work—our communication, our affection. That's no excuse, I know. But

I wanted to feel important. I wanted to feel fascinating. Amanda looked at me like I was the most interesting person she'd ever met. I didn't feel like that with you anymore. I felt like a co-parent."

"Okay, so, what changed? If you want to feel like someone's number one, why did you go down the parenting path with Emily?"

"Amanda was my bad girl, but it was never forever. And then I cheated on Amanda with some girl. And then a few more girls. I got it out of my system. Then I met Emily, and we clicked, and she wanted a baby. It's ironic. There have been many nights I wondered why I walked away from us to just do it all again. If I'd known what my future held, I don't think I'd have left us. I hate that I think that. It doesn't mean I don't love Emily and am not excited, but I'm repeating what we had with someone new." She gazed into the distance, and then caught Belle's eyes and blushed a little. "If I'd had a crystal ball at the time, if I'd seen the picket fence, the nappies and soccer mums, I'd have stayed and made it work with you. Brought back the magic. Made a really secure life for our girls. Maybe we'd be having the third child. If I'd known, I think I could have worked to make us work."

"I wish you had." Belle smiled sadly, but it also wasn't because of any pining for Tash. She completely understood what Tash was saying. They'd both moved on from "Belle and Tash" now, but she had always thought they could have made it work if Tash had been willing.

"It hasn't worked out so badly, though? We co-parent well. The girls know no different, and they're happy," Tash pondered aloud.

"I'm so proud of us too. It took us time, but here we are. I'm just sad that we won't be old and grey grandmothers together."

"We'll always be family, though. So we can still be old grannies together, just in a different way," Tash said. Then she added, "So you have it bad for Georgia? She's 100 per cent straight?"

"I was so determined I wasn't going to have another relationship, at least until the girls got older. And then I got blindsided. I thought it was just a nice friendship. Then I wondered if our connection was so strong because of the baby…"

"I wondered that. Maybe go out with a gay girl and see?"

"I did." Belle blushed. "I had a fling."

"Annabelle Andrews! You did not!"

"I did so," she laughed.

"And?"

"And it was fine…."

"Fine?" Tash looked sceptical. "Not exactly the word you want to use for a wild night of passion."

"Yeah. Fine. It was nice and all, but…"

"But it didn't light your fire? So? She's one girl. There are more. Don't set your sights on the straight girl. I know enough that it doesn't work out well. I had a liaison with a straight girl or two in my bad girl phase." Tash laughed. "Fun, indeed. But it's always going to end in heartbreak."

Belle looked intently at Tash. "What if she's not completely straight and hasn't realised? That happens all the time, doesn't it?"

"And that's the chance. You could plunge in, but from where I'm sitting, you have so much to lose. She's carrying your biological baby. Isn't it better to have a great friendship with her, see the baby, and jump into a relationship, or a fling, with someone else? This one is too risky."

"You were meant to make me feel ready to try." Belle grimaced.

"Well, I hope you do try with someone. I just don't know if it's safe with Georgia. I'm not one to shy away from what the heart tells you to do. You know that." Tash paused for a moment. "But this one is risky. If you go away, though, and think it's a risk you must take—if she's really the girl for you—then please don't live your life wondering. Talk to her and find out if there's a chance. If there's not, at least you won't spend a lifetime wondering."

"Maybe it is safer to just protect myself. I never thought I'd be here, ready to plunge in," Belle said.

Chapter Twenty-One

BELLE WALKED INTO the kitchen and grinned at Georgia, who had her twenty-four-week scan earlier that day.

"Hey," Georgia said.

"I'm so pleased for you that things are looking good."

"Nothing's changed, though. I'll still probably need a C-section."

"Maybe, but a C-section isn't the end of the world. I know it's not the ideal for you, but the most important thing is that the baby arrives safely."

Georgia's eyes filled with tears. "I know. And after all

I've been through, you'd think the birth is the least of my concerns." She shook her head. "It's stupid to even care. I have no idea if your mum had a vaginal birth or C-section with you, for starters."

Belle didn't offer up that her mum had had two very easy vaginal births. "True. In the end, it doesn't matter."

"Ugh, I sound like such a princess. Logically I know it doesn't matter, but I really wanted it to work out the way I'd imagined it all." The tears started flowing now, and Belle just wanted to fix things for her. She wished they had a crystal ball and could see into the future so that they could prepare. Georgia flipped the corn fritters sizzling in the fry pan and tried to hide her tears. "Anyway, I'll deal with it if it happens."

"Georgia, you don't have to hide how you're feeling with me. I know you're upset. It's best to let it out. I think it's best to deal with your feelings about this now, so that if you do end up having a C-section, you'll be prepared."

Georgia started to sob. "I'm so emotional; I don't know why."

"Because you're pregnant. I cried so much when I was

pregnant. I'm surprised you haven't been a blubbering mess every day." Belle stepped forward and embraced Georgia, who fell into the embrace. Belle stroked her long brown hair, and then held her by the waist and pulled her back to look at her. "Promise me you'll talk to me, though?"

Georgia nodded. "You're amazing. I couldn't do any of this without you. I bet you didn't think you signed up to being my support and housemate when you agreed to donate an embryo," she said, laughing through her tears.

Belle smiled, and then went to kiss her on the cheek, but Georgia moved at the last minute, and Belle's lips touched Georgia's. Georgia frowned in confusion but looked intently at Belle. Responding to the intense look, Belle kissed Georgia again, but this time directly on the lips, and passionately. Lust overcame her and she kissed Georgia as if her life depended on it. Georgia responded, making Belle feel weak at the knees—she'd always thought that expression was strange, but that kiss blew her mind.

Finally, after minutes of being lost in one another, Georgia pulled away, frowning at Belle. "Belle, I'm not... I'm not... This was a mistake." She looked overwhelmed and the tears started again.

Belle felt the pain of rejection, and instant confusion. She guessed Georgia was saying she wasn't interested, or maybe that she wasn't attracted to females, but Belle couldn't understand how she could think that and kiss her the way she'd just kissed her. An awkward dinner followed, and Belle went straight to her bedroom after dinner but did not manage to get any sleep all night.

She was out in the kitchen making a coffee early the next morning when Georgia sheepishly came out to the kitchen. "Belle," she said, awkwardly. "I'm sorry that I made you think…I…well… The scan went well, and I'm feeling good. It makes sense I go back home. Give you some space."

How could Belle have been so stupid? "No, it's all right. I won't…"

"I just think for both of us, the space could be good. I'll go home today, but we'll stay in touch."

Stay in touch? And with that, out walked the most amazing woman Belle had ever known. Through her stupidity, she had lost both her best friend and the baby she was carrying. She'd lost the connections with Georgia's family she'd made—she loved Jo in particular, but Georgia's mother, aunty, and the rest of the family seemed great too. Belle had looking forward to both of them becoming part of each other's extended families once the baby was born.

Belle sat on the couch and put her head into her hands. This was exactly the reason she'd not dated, not let herself become vulnerable to someone, and certainly the reason she'd never allowed herself to develop feelings for a straight girl. This pain she felt, this extreme longing, and this sadness were exactly what she hoped to never feel again. How could she get through all of this? She didn't want to admit her stupidity to Nikki, or Alex, or anyone for that matter. Certainly not her mother or Tash, who could both rightfully say "I told you so," but never would. Why had she put herself at risk again? There had been red flags, but she'd plunged in anyway.

*

THE NEXT WEEK felt like it was never going to end, but

things picked up once the girls arrived on Friday afternoon. Amazingly, Belle managed to have moments where she briefly forgot what had happened with Georgia, and in those moments, she felt like life was almost normal again. But soon enough, Belle would feel a nagging feeling, and suddenly she felt like the biggest idiot. How had she misread the situation so much to kiss her? She knew the issue was that she hadn't been thinking in the moment—she had simply reached out to try to make Georgia feel better, and she'd done what came naturally.

She was attracted to Georgia, but if she could take it all back and they could have salvaged some kind of friendship—as frustrating at that could be—she'd rather that. Now she'd lost everything. Now she possibly wouldn't even get to meet Georgia's baby, and she wouldn't ever get to spend time with Georgia, whom she adored spending time with. Even if Georgia took pity on her and let her meet the baby, or even be part of the baby's life, things between them would never be the same again. She had lost an incredible friendship.

*

THE FOLLOWING FRIDAY rolled around, and Belle dropped the girls to school. It was now Tash and Emily's turn to have their week with the girls. Though it wasn't what she'd ever have chosen and still came with mixed feelings, Belle usually enjoyed her week of *me* time. It was always nice to look forward to the breather from intense solo parenting. This time, though, she was anxious about the long week of being alone that stretched before her. She tried to distract herself, catching up with friends, going for a long walk, reading a book in the bath. It was hopeless, though. Time would be the only thing that would help her get Georgia off her mind. She just wondered how long.

The following week with the girls was very busy with birthday parties, play dates, and soccer matches. It felt like the whole week was crammed with after-school and weekend activities, and that pleased Belle just fine. While she normally might have been a little overwhelmed by the crazy week, she appreciated it as a distraction. On the Thursday night, soccer training was cancelled because of the rain, so they took advantage of it and had homemade pizza night.

It felt heart-warming and belly filling—a real soul food activity. They settled in for a movie in front of the television. Snuggling under blankets, Belle's phone buzzed. *Georgia.* All she wrote was:

> *Hey Belle, I hope you're going okay. I'm sorry about how things went between us. Would love to catch up some time.*

A pity text.

Belle put her phone down and tried to concentrate on the movie, but she'd now lost what was happening. The girls hadn't noticed.

She picked up her phone again and re-read it.

She put it down again and ended up having an early night once the movie had finished and the girls were in bed. She didn't get much sleep, though.

The next day, she dropped the girls at school—handover day once again. As she left the school, she decided it would be rude not to text Georgia, but she didn't know what to say. She simply wrote:

> *Hope you're going well.*

She hit send before she had time to rethink it and made her way to work.

Chapter Twenty-Two

IT WAS A busy day, jam-packed with back-to-back meetings, and Belle hardly found time to eat lunch or go to the bathroom. Given it was a Friday, though, everyone started to wind things up early.

"We're going to go for drinks," one of the young girls stated.

Belle barely knew her, and she was already exhausted after a long day, so probably wouldn't be the best company. She chastised herself—she really should start going to staff drinks, but she said that to herself often. This time she promised herself that in two weeks, she'd definitely go. She made her polite apologies—the rain, long day, the girls had worn her out—but she knew it just made her sound much older than her young, hip colleagues and very dowdy indeed. "Lindsay," she said, remembering the girl's name, "I'll definitely be there two weeks from now. You won't be able to stop me. Party time for me in two weeks."

Lindsay nodded politely and smiled thinly before leaving Belle's office doorway and heading off to ask someone else. Belle couldn't believe how pathetic she must seem. She worked in fashion and came across as some middle-aged mum—boring, exhausted, and frumpy. She was going home for a weekend of Netflix on the couch, after all. She rolled her eyes. Lindsay must be so pleased she wasn't coming to drinks, after all.

*

DODGING THE RAIN as much as she could, Belle put the key into the door and immediately threw her bag down and flopped on to the couch. She was exhausted, so she mindlessly put the television on. Her stomach had started to rumble, and she was just contemplating what to have for dinner when the doorbell stirred her thoughts. She frowned. It was a bit late and a bit wet for a door-to-door caller, so unless it was a persistent door-to-door caller, she had no idea. Friends didn't generally 'pop in' without notice. She opened the door and saw Georgia standing there.

"Hey," Belle said apprehensively.

Georgia went to speak, but Belle opened the door wide. "Come in—it's too wet to talk out there." Georgia's hair was drenched just from the walk from the driveway to the front door. "Towel?" Belle said, ready to walk to the linen closet.

Georgia shook her head. "I'm not one of those women that worries about wet hair." She shrugged. "I'm pretty low maintenance, actually. I may be a little crazy at times—I love nothing more than loud music on a Saturday morning. I usually clean to it as I belt out a tune. I live my life as if there's a soundtrack playing in my head—I can turn anything into a song. But my singing is bad. Luckily, I have a different day job. I am a little too devoted to my students and sometimes don't get home from work until dinner time. Some nights I'm too exhausted to cook, and I make cheese toasties. Some weeks I live on them, especially as I'm writing report cards. I definitely don't wear matching pyjamas to bed, unless it's my thick onesie in the middle of winter, which I'm obsessed with. My farts stink—a lot. Jo reckons they linger in a room for hours. And I'm incredibly regular with my number twos; you can almost set a clock by them." Georgia laughed a little. "I'm awful at buying surprise gifts. I'd much rather someone tell me directly what they want. So, I buy fairly boring gifts and rely too much on gift vouchers. Oh, and I rehearse a lot of my speeches, like they're lines in a movie, but they seem to come out better in front of my mirror than they do in real life."

Belle's eyes narrowed in confusion. She didn't understand why Georgia was telling her all of this. Before she asked, though, Georgia spoke again. "I've been here for weeks, as a guest, doing all the right things. You haven't smelt my farts. We haven't shared a bathroom. I've cooked nice dinners when you haven't. If we're going to be a couple, you need to know who I am when I'm not on my best behaviour. Because if we do this"—she shook her head and stretched out her hands—"I don't want you to change your mind. Because if we do this, eventually you'll be having a cheese toasty for dinner some night."

Belle stared at Georgia, wanting to be certain she'd just heard what she thought she'd heard. "Back up. Be a couple? Do this? But you're not…"

"I don't know what I am, to be honest. I've never thought about it, and I guess that could be a deal-breaker for you. All I know is that getting to know you over the past few months has been the happiest time of my life. All I know is that since I've left, I haven't been able to stop thinking about you. And that kiss. Jo's a little worried it's because of the baby." She touched her stomach as she spoke. "But it's not. It's you, Belle Andrews." She smiled, "I missed you. And I want… Us…"

"Are you sure?" Belle didn't dare to hope that this wasn't some kind of practical joke or miscommunication, but Georgia stepped forward, embraced Belle, and kissed her, gently at first, and then passionately.

"I've been thinking about doing that since the night I left," she said, smiling softly.

Belle nodded. "Me too. But I've been heartbroken."

"I'm sorry. I needed time. I felt it, too, the whole time, actually, but I was scared. And then I realised…"

Belle bit her lip. "I don't know, Georgia. You walked out so easily… I've decided I would prefer friendship than nothing. Isn't it safer to not…?"

Georgia nodded. "It's far safer… I agree. But I think we have to take the plunge. Safe is what we were doing. But now… I've missed you so much."

"What have you missed? Our friendship?"

Georgia twirled her hair around her finger. "It's more than friendship, I know that, and we saw that when you kissed me. My God, I've never been kissed like that before… I wondered if maybe it was a fluke, but then we just kissed again, and it certainly wasn't a fluke. It's us!" Belle searched Georgia's face for the answers. "Belle. Don't overthink it. Please? Let's just feel. We've been overthinking for the past few weeks."

"I've spent the last few years overthinking, actually," Belle admitted. "But I don't ever want to get hurt the way Tash hurt me. And you're pregnant, and… Well, it's hardly straightforward."

Belle's mind was reeling. Here, Georgia was offering her what she'd been pining for and dreaming of for months, and yet, it was so risky. Plunging forward could be wonderful, or it could bring a heartbreak bigger than anything she'd ever experienced before—no Georgia, and no baby. A second heartbreak would certainly mean the end of her, emotionally. She simply couldn't do it. Then again, Tash had now explained that their break-up wasn't due to any major fault Belle had, but because they'd started their relationship so young. It was itchy feet for Tash. Georgia was in a totally different place. There were never any guarantees, anyway. Maybe it was worth trying.

But what if it wasn't? Georgia was looking at her waiting for her to speak.

"I just don't know," Belle finally admitted. "I'm so scared. You were never even attracted to women…"

Georgia laughed, "I know. It's crazy. At least I never knew I was attracted to women, but I am now. And remember when I said to the counsellor I was curious when I saw you at that party, after Michael and I broke up? When you were in the long white dress? That part was not acting. I did wonder back then. I was attracted to you then. I really was, but I didn't understand. I'm definitely attracted to at least one woman. One amazing woman. And that's why I'm saying let's not overthink. Let's just…be."

Belle couldn't believe what she was hearing and was feeling a little breathless. "You really want to? You really want everything that comes with it all? You want to be a couple, or do you just want a fling?"

Georgia smiled. "I want it all. I can't think of anything more perfect."

They kissed again, and again. Finally Belle grinned. "I can't believe this. What terrible timing, when we can't—"

"Yes, I'm still on pelvic rest." She raised her eyebrows, clearly reading what Belle was thinking.

Belle laughed, embarrassed. "Oh well. At least we're together. Let's grab some takeaway and then spend the night snuggling in bed. Actually, let's take the takeaway menus in there," Belle said, leading her towards the bedroom.

*

BELLE STIRRED IN the morning and noticed Georgia, awake, lying with her arms around her. "Hey." Belle grinned. "I wondered if this was all a dream, or if I'd wake up and you were gone, or…"

"Shh." Georgia put her finger over her mouth in a shushing motion. "Stop overthinking, remember?"

Belle rolled toward Georgia, running her hands between her breasts and tracing the outline of her growing belly. "Your tummy is all baby. When I was pregnant, it was only half baby and half Doritos." Belle joked, but she was only exaggerating a little.

"Now, what are we doing today?" Georgia asked.

"Well, it's meant to rain all weekend. I vote we stay in bed and watch movies all weekend."

"Sloth!" Georgia teased Belle. "I was thinking a movie, hand in hand, or maybe we could go to Jo's to catch up. She often has a barbeque." Belle pulled the blind out so she could get a glimpse out of the window. "I'm not going to a backyard barbie, but I'm happy to socialise, providing you stay with me tonight too."

"I wouldn't stay anywhere else," Georgia said.

Chapter Twenty-Three

HOURS LATER, IT was arranged that Georgia would meet Jo, and Belle would meet Nikki at the movies. "We could have some fun with this," Belle had said. "Making out like it was just a catch up for two."

Georgia caught on quickly. "Maybe we could pretend we ran into one another."

"And then just start kissing," Belle said.

"Maybe that's too cruel to our best friends," Georgia suggested with a twinkle in her eye, but they decided to do it anyway.

Belle met Nikki at a coffee shop around the corner of the cinema, while Georgia and Jo arranged to meet at the cinema. They were already standing in line to buy tickets when Belle and Nikki walked into the cinema.

"Oh my gosh, there's Georgia and Jo," Nikki whispered to Belle. "Are you okay?"

Belle glanced in their direction and then responded to Nikki, "Wow, her stomach is getting big."

"That's what happens. Will you be okay? We can leave. What if they're seeing what we're—?"

At that point, Jo called out, "Belle, hi. Nikki, hi. You aren't seeing the Renee Zellweger movie, are you? We are."

Nikki cringed and squeezed Belle's hand in support. Belle almost cracked up laughing. "We are," Belle responded.

"Oh, we hadn't really decided, had we? We were going to look to see what's out," Nikki said casually. She was clearly trying to offer support to Belle in case being in the vicinity of Georgia was too much.

"Yes, I'm dying to see it," Belle protested. She then grinned at Georgia. "How are you?"

"Good. Very good."

"Not too tired?"

"No." She smiled.

"It's just, you're pretty pregnant now. That's tiring. Plus, I kept you up pretty late last night…" Belle's comment was loaded, and Nikki and Jo shot confused looks between themselves, and then toward Belle and Georgia.

"Huh?" Jo finally blurted out, and Georgia cracked up laughing.

"Belle and I are here together." Her eyes were twinkling in delight as she spoke.

"As in together, together?" Nikki frowned in confusion. "But you're not…?"

Georgia shrugged and waved her hand as if to dismiss the matter. "I can work that out later. Maybe I'm gay, maybe I'm bi, maybe I'm just a Bellosexual." She laughed.

"That's so corny." Jo shook her head. "Please don't let it be that one, and please don't ever say that again. Ever. Again." She pretended to puke, and everyone laughed.

"To be honest, I've never felt this way. So, whatever it is, it's making me really happy and that's worth it."

Ever the sage older cousin, Jo raised her eyebrows towards Belle. "I've already welcomed you to the family, but I have one important question." Everyone gave Jo their attention. "You said you kept her up all night, but doctor's orders were very clear—"

Belle blushed. "We stayed up all night talking and cuddling. That's it."

"God, you're losing your touch," Nikki quipped.

Belle shrugged. "For so many reasons, I cannot wait until this baby is born."

*

AFTER THE MOVIE, the four women had lunch together, which was just as effortless as it had previously been, but they had more to laugh about. "Are you moving back in?" Nikki asked. "Or...?" She trailed off, leaving the option open.

Georgia looked at Belle and then back to Nikki and Jo. "To be honest, we haven't properly discussed it. I just want to be with her." Georgia had said to Belle the night before that she didn't want to intrude on Belle's life—she seemed to have a good routine between time with the girls and her alone time. If Georgia moved in, her week alone would be no longer, and soon enough there would be another child.

"We don't want to U-Haul," Belle said. "But she was living with me until she disappeared."

"Disappeared?" Jo said, looking confused. "I thought you went home to think."

"I didn't tell you everything," Georgia said, blushing. "The morning I left Belle's house wasn't as well planned as I might have made out. I ran away."

Jo looked even more confused, and Belle spoke up. "I think I scared her off." She laughed a little nervously. "I kissed her. And it wasn't a peck."

Jo's eyebrows raised. "Oh." She directed her conversation to her cousin. "So that's how you knew Belle was interested?" She then turned to Belle and Nikki to explain. "She told me she had feelings for you, and was working through them, but I kept saying, 'Just because she's gay doesn't mean she'll want you. You don't even know how Belle feels about you.' Clearly she did." Jo smiled. "Oh my gosh, have you told your mum?"

Georgia shook her head. "I suppose I should."

"Absolutely you should," Jo said.

"Don't tell your mum first," Georgia warned her cousin.

"As if I would. You need your mum to know first."

"What do you think she'll think?" Belle asked. "I think she likes me."

"She does like you. A lot." Georgia nodded. "She told me that after she met you. Whether she likes you as her daughter's partner remains to be seen," she grinned, "but we'll soon find out."

Belle couldn't believe how self-assured Georgia was in her 'coming out.' Belle had cried the entire time in the lead-up to her coming out, but of course she was just a teenager. Still, it was a big deal for people, regardless of how old they were. Georgia's comfort about it relaxed Belle. Maybe Georgia had really reflected on it all before coming back to Belle and was ready to come out and live her life in a partnership of two women.

As they left the lunch, Georgia said, "Want to pop into Mum's together? Jo's right; we really should tell her."

Belle grimaced. "You don't think you should do that one alone?"

Georgia thought it over. "Good point. It'll be a bit of a surprise for Mum."

They agreed that Georgia would drop into her mum's and Belle would visit her parents. Belle's mother was already suspecting something was going on, so she wouldn't be surprised.

Belle rang the doorbell and thought she probably should have told her parents she was coming and check they were home. Just as she was wondering if they were even home, her dad came to the door. "Belle, everything okay?" Belle wasn't well-known for impromptu pop-ins.

She nodded. "Just thought I'd come and say g'day. Where's Mum?"

"She's in the backyard; we're getting the pool ready for summer."

Belle and her father walked through the house, to the backyard. Her mother was sweeping the bottom of the pool. "Oh, hi, love," Julie said. "I didn't know you were dropping over."

Belle shrugged. "I just thought I'd pop in."

"You okay?" Her mother looked worried. Belle offered a hand with the pool. Her father handed her a net to get any loose leaves, while he tidied up around the pool area. Belle was secretly relieved they all had something to keep them occupied while they talked.

"I just wanted to let you know that Georgia and I are together now."

"Together? As in dating?" Clive asked.

"Actually, we've not done any dating. We just talked last night." She blushed thinking that they hadn't actually talked much, but she wasn't going to say that to her parents. "I probably should take her on a date."

Julie nodded. "You should. You're her first girlfriend, aren't you?"

"Yes." Belle sighed. She was thrilled to be with Georgia but really hoped that Georgia was certain about all of this.

"It'll be okay," her mother said, reading her mind. "She seems really happy around you. And, oh, wow, she's having a baby soon." Her mum puffed out her cheeks in exasperation. "Talk about starting slow." She laughed.

"Yes, a new baby soon—you better get those dates in soon," Clive said.

"Maybe we should go away for a weekend. Some time away from it all before we have the baby. That might be nice."

Her mother agreed. "Yes, you don't have long. Dad and I'll be happy to babysit any time, of course, but I'm sure you and Georgia won't want that for a while. Oh, Clive, a new baby in the family. I'm so excited to have a new grandchild."

Clive smiled. "Of course, she's been calling it her grandchild ever since she heard it was on the way, even before you and Georgia were together." Clive and Belle shared an amused look with one another, their eyes twinkling, and Julie gently wacked Clive.

"You can laugh," she said, "but I must have had a sixth sense about this." Her mother put the broom down and turned to Clive. "Two daughters announcing relationships on the one day. I did not expect that this morning."

Belle's brow creased. "What? Alex?"

"Yes, love, unless I have another daughter I don't know

about."

"Alex is in a relationship?"

"Yes, love. She said she'd call in on you on the way home, but maybe she missed you. Now I've gone and told you."

"Not Anton?"

Her mother grinned. "They got together in New Zealand. They seem really happy too."

"Oh wow. That's...surprising after all this time."

"Surprising but lovely. I'm so happy for them," Julie said, and Clive and Belle agreed.

*

TURNED OUT MARY was thrilled for Georgia too. She told Belle all about it when she got home. Apparently, Mary had said, "Oh, I do like that girl." Georgia said she had clarified they were a couple, and not just friends. Her mother had apparently said, "Oh, Georgia, I wasn't born yesterday. You said you had gotten together with Belle. I know what that means. And I like that girl. I'm happy if you're happy."

"It was the easiest coming out in the history of the

world," Georgia said. "She likes you, and she wants us to come over for a meal sometime soon."

"That sounds lovely," Belle said.

Chapter Twenty-Four

ON SATURDAY AFTERNOON, Belle and Georgia were at a coast retreat, enjoying the warm spring day. They'd dined out after arriving Friday night, strolled by the harbourside, had brunch, and gone to a movie in the morning, and were now sitting relaxing on the balcony overlooking the ocean.

"This is wonderful," Georgia said.

"It's perfect, isn't it?" Belle said, grinning.

"Yes, I feel very lucky to get whisked away to such a gorgeous place." They sat in happy silence, just enjoying the sounds of the ocean.

"Do you have a bucket list? Places you want to go, or anything?" Georgia finally asked.

"Not really. I did a lot of travel in my twenties," Belle said. "What about you?"

"I haven't travelled as much. I had my first international trip a few years ago, and now I usually try to do something each year during school holidays, whether that's international or local. Now we'll have a baby, so I guess long distance travel won't be on my agenda for a while."

"You can travel with kids, though. It's different, but still possible."

Georgia nodded. "How do you and Tash work holidays with the week on, week off?"

"If you want to go somewhere with the kids for longer than your allocated week, we just swap days. If you want to go away kid-free for longer than the week, that's possible too. Tash and Amanda spent a month in Asia when they were together. Tash and I are good like that, which is nice."

"We should write a list of places we'd like to go together, then."

"That's a great idea. If you're ever at the point that

you're ready to leave the baby home, my parents would be happy babysitters. I reckon even Tash and Emily would look after the baby with the girls some time. I think we've got a lot of support."

Georgia smiled. "Plus my mum. She's so happy for us. And Jo and Sarah, and Aunty Susan. We're surrounded by people, really." She rubbed her belly. "But I don't think I'll be keen to have a child-free break just yet."

"Just wait for the terrible twos." Belle laughed. "Maybe then."

Georgia walked from the bedroom to the shower, dropping her towel in the doorway to the bathroom. Belle glanced at her, feeling strange about looking, and yet, couldn't look away—her full breasts, her curving stomach, her long, lean legs. "You're killing me, Georgia." She blushed. Now that they'd become a couple, living together, sharing a bed together, and stealing kisses all the time, not being able to be physically intimate was near impossible. Being away on a romantic 'babymoon' seemed to make it even harder. Belle didn't know if it was the world's longest torture, or the world's longest foreplay she was experiencing. She joked to Georgia that she was the one needing the shower—a cold one. Georgia simply shook her head, perhaps not realising the full effect she had on Belle.

A little while later, Georgia appeared out of the bedroom, dressed for dinner. She wore a tight black dress, a coloured kimono jacket, and black ankle boots. Her growing belly was accentuated by the fitted dress. Red lipstick completed the look, and her light brown hair flowed in gentle waves over her shoulders. "You look gorgeous," Belle said, kissing Georgia on the lips.

"So do you," Georgia responded.

Belle was wearing her standard skinny jeans, with a red button-up shirt, red boots, and her long dark hair was tied up in a ponytail. "Thanks."

They wandered down to the waterside, looking at the menus of the various restaurants, before settling on a small Italian bistro that looked joyful.

Georgia ordered the beef lasagne, and Belle opted for a creamy bacon pasta. "This is so nice," Georgia said, pointing to her dinner. "And I've been so hungry. I really do feel like I'm eating for two at the moment." After dinner, they kept strolling along the waterside, stumbling across an ice creamery. They had generous serves of ice cream, and then walked back to their beach cabin, hand in hand. Georgia smiled as she cocked her head toward Belle. "I never once imagined my life turning out like this, but it's perfect. I honestly couldn't be happier."

"Really?" Belle asked. There was a small part of her worried that the pregnancy hormones were making her want to be partnered up and that, somehow, she'd give birth and wonder what on earth she was thinking.

"Absolutely." Georgia smiled. "You are my person, without a doubt." Then, in the moonlight, Belle smiled down at Georgia, and moved in to eliminate the distance between them. She kissed Georgia gently, and Georgia responded. They then walked up the stairs and unlocked the door to their apartment, still hand in hand. "I'm so full, but what a perfect evening," Georgia said.

"Did you want to watch a movie or something?"

"I'm feeling a bit achy now. I wouldn't mind lying down in bed. If you want to come with me, we could lay and talk."

"If I want to come with you." Belle laughed. "Of course I do. I don't want to be apart from you for a minute this weekend."

They went into the bedroom, and Belle put her pyjamas on. Georgia slid her bra off, but under her dress, keeping the black dress on. "It's comfortable." She brushed the dress down. "And I don't have many PJs that fit anymore."

They got into bed, and talked about everything and nothing, while Belle traced her fingers up and down Georgia's bare arms. Goosebumps appeared. "Are you ticklish?" Belle asked her.

"Not particularly, but you're tickling me, anyway."

Belle kept tracing her, until Georgia finally pinned her hands behind her. She started to kiss her, gently and playfully at first, until Belle responded to Georgia's kisses, and finally they were kissing one another, matching each other's rhythm. Belle sighed. Gradually, Georgia started to move her mouth all over Belle's face, and finally her neck and then her ear. After moaning for some time, Belle said, "Georgia, doing that…what you're doing…my neck…my ear… It really turns me on. It's a bit dangerous right now."

"I like turning you on," Georgia said, grinning, but not stopping.

"That's good that you do, and we have all the time for that when we can…err…see it through to the end. For now, let's be sensible. I'm dying here."

Georgia ended up giving in to Belle's request, though she did tease her for being a spoilsport. "Besides, I could always turn you on and take it further. *You're* not on pelvic rest," she added.

"I know." Belle grimaced. "And believe me, the thought has crossed my mind, but I really want your first time…our first time…to be special. So, let's not do a half-hearted attempt now. Let's wait until you've got the all clear too."

"It might not be until the baby's born, and then we'll have no time for that." Georgia sulked.

"Believe me, we'll make time." Belle laughed. "I'll make sure of that."

*

THEIR LAST DAY of their weekend away was spent with

more dining out—a beautiful breakfast overlooking the waterfront—then a stroll along the waterside, before the drive home. "I think we have time to cram another one of these weekends away in before the baby's here," Georgia said. "It was just what I needed."

"I don't know. I don't think we should travel too far away towards the end of the pregnancy. Let's wait and see how things are."

"Good idea. I hadn't thought of that. We can plan a staycation. Maybe you could take a couple of days off work, and we just relax at home or something like that."

"That sounds perfect."

"Hey, I enjoyed this weekend away so much," Georgia said. "I've been thinking. How would you feel if I brought Oscar over to live with us?"

Belle loved the idea. It meant that Georgia wouldn't be going anywhere if her cat was moving in. "What about your stuff?"

Georgia looked closely at Belle. "I thought it might be good to rent my place out. Your place is much bigger, and it makes sense for us to officially live together with the baby on the way. Unless you think it's too soon?"

"We haven't been apart anyway. I think it sounds perfect with a baby on the way."

*

A FEW WEEKS later, just as Belle and Georgia were getting ready to go to the doctors for a prenatal appointment, Belle received a phone call. "Can you come into the office?" her boss asked her. "We got the proofs from the photo shoot and need to make some calls on the imagery to go to print."

As she started to respond, she must have looked torn, because Georgia was shaking her head and gesturing. "Go, it's okay."

"Let me just check something," Belle said into the phone, then covered it.

"It's fine. Go into work. I can go alone. These appointments are so brief."

"Are you sure?"

Georgia agreed, and then Belle agreed to meet her boss in half an hour.

She got off the phone and whined, "But it's a

Saturday." She flopped into a chair, very unimpressed.

"Yes, and you've said yourself you have flexibility, but there's give and take. Go now and we'll both be back before lunch time."

"Okay," she said unconvincingly, but she finally got up and rushed out the door, knowing that the sooner she got there and back, the sooner she'd be home for a quiet afternoon in with Georgia.

*

LATER THAT AFTERNOON, Belle was in the bedroom putting her laundry away when Georgia came rushing in. "Tash just called. They're dropping the girls here. Emily's going to hospital."

Belle was thrilled. Emily's birth meant they were so much closer to Georgia having the baby.

"Oh cool. Are they okay?" Belle said, abandoning the laundry.

"I'm not sure." Emily was only thirty-eight weeks pregnant, which was early, but definitely not too early.

When they arrived, Tash looked anything but okay,

and Emily was waiting in the car. Belle and Georgia walked out to the car and Emily looked very pale. "When did labour start?"

Tash shook her head. "She's not in labour. She has pre-eclampsia; we only found out a few days ago. They thought she'd just be fine, given it's so late in the pregnancy, but the hospital just called, and her tests aren't good; she needed to rush up."

"Oh, shit, are you okay?"

Emily looked pale as she spoke. "I don't know. I hope so, but they think I won't be leaving hospital without a baby."

Belle and Georgia wished them well and told them to let them know if they needed anything. "I hope we'll be okay," Tash said, but Belle had never seen her look so anxious.

She gave her a hug, and said, "Don't worry about the girls; we're happy to have them for as long as you need us to."

"Appreciate that. Thanks," Tash said.

Hours later, Tash's name popped up on the screen of

Belle's phone. Belle walked out of earshot of the girls, in case the news wasn't good, but thankfully the news was positive. "Em had an emergency C-section, but they're doing well. Our baby is here. It's a girl. Three daughters."

"Oh, congratulations!" Belle said excitedly. "Has she got a name yet?'

"Sophia Ann," Tash said.

"Oh, beautiful. I can't wait to meet her. Let us know when Emily is up to visitors. I'm sure the girls would love to meet their sister."

Only three hours later, Belle and Georgia took the girls up to meet their baby sister. There was a lot of excited chatter in the car, and they found their way to the hospital room. Knocking as they entered, the girls excitedly burst into the room but turned shy when they met the baby. They sat with Tash for some time before they finally gave Sophia a cuddle and posed for many photographs. Belle quickly sent a few to her family to share pictures of the girls meeting their sister.

"I wonder whether you'll have a boy or girl," Tash said, glancing at Georgia who'd mostly stood back.

"I can't tell. I keep changing my mind," Georgia said. Belle put her arm gently around Georgia's back, and Tash noticed, but didn't say anything.

After a while, Belle started to pack up their things. "I suppose we'll be going and let you settle in together as a family. Girls," she said, directing her words to them. They looked up. "Let's head home, and let Mum and Emily settle in with Sophia." As they went to walk out, Tash followed them out.

While Georgia was busy chatting to the girls on the walk to the car, Tash managed a quiet word with Belle. "Are you two...?"

Belle nodded, smiling.

"You look happy. Well done. What does it mean for the baby?"

Belle shrugged. She actually had no idea what role she'd play in the life of the baby, and strangely, she was okay to wait and see how that all evolved. Her attraction to Georgia wasn't about the baby, although she was excited to be part of the baby's life.

"I'm really happy for you," Tash said seriously.

"Thanks, and I'm really happy for you too." The two women embraced. "Congratulations. Sophia is beautiful."

"We're thrilled. Let me know when the girls want to visit again."

"Based on their excitement, I'm sure you'll see us again tomorrow."

"Thanks, Belle. I hope so."

Chapter Twenty-Five

"OH MY GOSH," Georgia said once the girls were tucked into bed that evening. "I'd forgotten how small babies are. I can't believe we're going to have one of those soon."

"You're going to have one of those soon," Belle corrected her instinctively.

Georgia frowned and looked a little offended. When she spoke, her voice was higher pitched than usual. "Well, aren't we a couple?"

"Yes, but..." Belle didn't know what to say. She'd spent so long telling herself it was Georgia's baby, and that she had no claim over the baby. She wondered if it was different just because they were having a romantic relationship. Would it be different if she wasn't the biological mother of the baby? Finally, Belle spoke up. "Would you consider it our baby if I wasn't the embryo donor? We didn't set out to do this together. I don't want you to think that it's changed just because we're together."

"Well, Belle, I guess I thought that it had changed. And I thought we were on the same page, believing that biology didn't matter, so yes, even if you weren't the embryo donor, you'd be in this with me. You got into a relationship with a pregnant woman—I'm kind of a package deal at this point." She pointed to her very pregnant belly and laughed a little. "Besides, I don't have plans to be anywhere else, do you?"

Belle was now worried she'd both offended Georgia and over-emphasised the importance of biology. She didn't know what to say, but she finally spoke up. "I want to do it together, but I don't want you to think you owe me anything because you set out to do this as a single mum."

"Do you think I wanted to, though? I started this with Mike, but as desperate as I was for a baby, in the end I was pleased it didn't work with him. And then I was so heart-broken when it didn't work solo with a sperm donor. I thought it meant I'd never get to be a mum." She was now in tears. "I thought that was it. My dream was over. But now I know why. This led me to you. We were meant to have this baby together. I can't force you to stay, and I can't force you to be this baby's other mother, but I'm not going to…" Georgia struggled to speak, then finally added, "I'm not going to walk away from the person that's made me the happiest I've ever been just because of…fear! Or whatever it is that you're experiencing."

"Oh, Georgia. I'm scared of being vulnerable. I've been so hurt before. I spent my entire adult life building everything with Tash. I now know that not everything lasts forever and I'm not pining for Tash, but it was hard to move on. But I also know this feels right. I'm not scared. I just don't want to be presumptuous. I just don't want to stake claim on your child. As for not going anywhere… I'm a one-woman woman, and I'm proudly your woman."

"That's good, Annabelle, because I love you."

"You love me?" Belle asked, tears in her eyes.

Georgia grinned, "I do. I'm in love with you."

"I love you too," Belle said. "So much."

Georgia lent over to Belle and kissed her—gently at first, but then more intimately. She stood up and led Belle to the bedroom. She lay next to Belle and kept kissing her. The kissing was turning Belle on too much, and Georgia's sighing told Belle that she felt the same way.

"We should go to sleep," Belle said. She didn't want them to get carried away again.

"Sleep is not part of my plan," Georgia said as she ignored Belle and kept kissing her. Belle tried to pull away, but Georgia got closer. Soon, she started to unbutton Belle's top, and instantly Belle wanted to both encourage her and push her away at the same time. Georgia broke their kiss and started to kiss Belle's neck and ear. Belle had already warned Georgia how much this turned her on. Georgia was playing such a dangerous game, but Belle no longer cared. It felt so good, and she figured a little longer wouldn't hurt. She could always stop it later. Next, Georgia snapped open Belle's bra and started to caress and kiss her breasts. As she took a nipple into her mouth, and sucked it, Belle bucked in excitement underneath Georgia.

"I think you better...stop." She moaned lightly. If Georgia kept going, she'd be tipped over the edge, and that was hardly fair. But Georgia didn't stop, and soon Belle was moaning in ecstasy as Georgia expertly feasted on her breasts.

"I'm so sorry," Belle panted. "I didn't expect that."

"Why are you sorry?" Georgia asked innocently. "I enjoyed every moment of that."

Belle was surprised when Georgia kept trailing her hand all over her, finally landing between her legs. "No," Belle protested. "No, no, I won't let you do that."

Georgia instead straddled Belle and kept kissing her. "That shut you up," she laughed. Once Belle was finally quiet, Georgia trailed her kisses down the length of Belle's body and stopped between her legs. S

"Can I touch you, please?" Georgia asked, and finally, Belle agreed. Georgia traced one finger between her thighs. Belle was very wet, and very ready, so Georgia used the tip of her finger to trail up and down, increasing the intensity as she rubbed. Belle sighed, moved her hips in a circular motion.

Georgia placed a single finger inside her. Belle never felt so ready but knew that she couldn't return the favour and it wasn't what she had wanted. It was too late to protest further because it felt so good. Suddenly Georgia was exploring Belle, inserting fingers, rubbing her, and occasionally using her tongue. Belle's hips bucked, and her moans got louder and louder, as she was brought to ecstasy again and again.

"Wow," she said, afterwards. "You're damn good at that."

"My first time," Georgia said, proudly.

"You're a natural." Belle bit her lip, as she traced her fingers down Georgia's stomach. "My only disappointment is that I can't return the favour." Belle loved what they'd just experienced but felt awful for Georgia and she promised herself she wouldn't let Georgia get her carried away again like that until they were free to continue.

Georgia grinned cheekily. "Remember I saw the doctor this morning?"

Belle nodded.

"I got the all clear."

"You got the all clear… Does that mean the placenta…?"

"Please don't talk about placentas right now. I'll update you later. In the meantime, I'm all yours if you still want to return the favour."

Belle couldn't believe Georgia hadn't told her when she'd got back from the doctor, but she didn't let herself dwell on that for too long. Instead, she lay beside Georgia—recognising that Georgia's bump was a little in the way between them—and started to kiss her. She began to nibble Georgia's ear instinctively and realised that really turned Georgia on, and her moaning was getting louder. Belle gently trailed her fingers over Georgia's swollen breasts. She couldn't resist gently kissing them, and finally, she kissed over her bulging stomach, and found her way between Georgia's legs. Georgia's hips were already bucking in excitement, and she was already so wet from turning Belle on so much.

Belle placed her mouth on her, and started licking—softly at first, finally flicking Georgia's hard clitoris with her tongue. Georgia grew wetter under Belle's tongue and Belle eagerly lapped it up. Georgia spread her legs wide, and Belle placed two fingers inside her, moving them around while she licked. Georgia wailed in pleasure, bucking her hips against Belle's face, and after tensing her legs, she wrapped them around Belle's head. Belle was so turned on by Georgia's response to her that the second time Georgia came, Belle did too at the same time, even though she wasn't being touched herself.

Georgia's moans were so intense, the most intense Belle had ever witnessed, that she wondered if it was because she had been denied so long, because it was her first time with a woman, or whether that was just the intensity of Georgia's orgasms. She knew that pregnancy could result in more intense orgasms, so maybe it was that. She silently vowed to herself to spend the next eight weeks taking advantage of it.

Belle woke the following day before Georgia. She rolled over and stroked Georgia, but just lightly, not enough to wake her. She needed her sleep. Belle smiled, but her mind wandered. They'd had the most incredible evening, but how would Georgia feel now? Was she certain, now, about her feelings and attraction for Belle, or would she wake up filled with regret for how far she'd gone? Belle suspected Georgia was just as interested as she was—she knew she hadn't been acting the night before, it was the real deal—but she couldn't help but worry. Georgia had never been attracted to women before. What if this was some kind of hormonal thing? Or something to do with the embryo donation? Belle chastised herself—the night before had been amazing. A connection like that doesn't come along often, Belle knew, and she needed to stop second-guessing it.

As if on cue, Georgia woke, smiled, and cuddled into Belle, silencing any of her fears. Still, Belle spoke up, joking about her worries. "I thought you might wake up and say 'nice night, thanks for that, but no thanks.'"

Georgia frowned and looked serious. "Did you really worry about that? I thought I made it pretty clear last night how I felt." She broke into a smile, and Belle smiled back. Georgia reached over and pecked Belle on the lips.

"I guess it just seemed too good to be true."

"Well, you better get used to the idea. You've got another baby on the way," Georgia said, laughing. "There's no time to overthink. We've got a lot of organising to do."

*

WHEN SOPHIA WAS about two weeks old, Cora and Ada finally returned to their normal family rotation schedule. Belle had offered to drop the children off, both as a convenience for Tash and Emily, who were both on parental leave from work, but also to get another chance to see Sophia.

"She's adorable," Belle said, holding the baby. "Isn't your sister so cute?"

Cora and Ada nodded. "I want to hold her," Ada said. Belle looked at Tash, leaving her to answer.

"It might be best to cuddle her once you've had your showers and we're having some quiet time before bed."

The girls agreed and raced off to play with their toys.

"The girls will be well-trained in baby handling by the time your baby comes along," Tash said, laughing.

Belle agreed. "They'll be great big sisters between Sophia and the next one."

"It'd be crazy if you have another girl too. Cora and Ada having two more sisters." Tash smiled. "Whatever it is, they'll be doting big sisters.

Chapter Twenty-Six

THE NEXT FEW weeks seemed to be a whirlwind of kids'
activities, doctors' check-ups for Georgia, and social events
with various friends and family. Between it all, Belle pushed
herself to get all her planning done for the new year so that
she could take some time off once the baby arrived. Her
boss, Simone, had been quite surprised at her request to take
parental leave for a third child—a child Simone had not expected. In the evenings, Belle and Georgia basked in one another's company and made up for lost time every chance
they got. Life was going well.

Two days before Christmas, Belle was out in the garden planting herbs and vegie seeds when Georgia came outside. She'd been relaxing inside. "How did your labours start?"

"Oh gosh, George. I've told you the stories a million times—where I was, how long it took."

"But you didn't really tell me how you knew. The first pains. Was it a strange back pain and like a period pain?"

"Yeah, it was actually." Belle kept digging, and then she suddenly put the shovel down. "Are you saying...?"

Georgia's face seemed to show a strange mixture of excitement and a small grimace of pain. "It's here, and here." She pointed to her lower back and her pelvis. "It feels like the worst period I've ever had. And then it goes, and then it returns."

"Shit, let's go inside. You can sit up on the couch, watch a movie, and time them."

After getting advice from the midwife and spending hours relaxing at home, the two women made the call to go to the hospital. Tash and Emily had the girls, which was one thing they didn't have to worry about. Belle was always a bit sad when she didn't have the girls for Christmas, but now, she was relieved.

Once they'd arrived at the hospital and were waiting for a check-up, they let their families know. "Can we come up?" both mothers asked.

"Well, I wouldn't rush it," Belle said. "There's no real point. We could be days away."

"Oh, a Christmas Day baby could be on the cards," Belle's mother said. Belle said they certainly hoped that wasn't the case. "If it's Christmas Day, you'll still make the child's birthday special," Julie said to Belle.

"Of course, but hopefully it'll happen sooner. Georgia's in a lot of pain."

The next few hours were spent with regular checks, walking around the hospital, and lots of agony and discomfort from Georgia. "You're progressing well," the midwife said. "Just keep doing what you're doing." Georgia looked like she was going to thump her.

It became obvious that the baby wouldn't be born until at least the next day—a Christmas Eve baby. Georgia kept asking if it would really take that long, and the midwives said unfortunately it would. "I can't keep going," Georgia cried out. "I'm not going to."

Belle grinned at her. "What's the alternative, babe?"

Despite the pain, the labour was mostly unremarkable, and hours later, Georgia was ready to push. Belle spent the entire time up next to Georgia, being her personal cheerleader and encouraging her to keep pushing and breathing through her pain. As the baby started to descend, she raced down to the 'business end' to watch the baby crowning.

"Oh, wow, lots of hair!" Belle yelled up to Georgia. Georgia said it explained the heartburn she'd experienced. It was an old wives' tale but seemed to have some truth to it. The baby was pulled out by the doctor, and the doctor did a quick glance. In a matter of seconds, the baby was placed on Georgia's chest for skin-to-skin contact. "It's a boy!" Belle announced.

"A boy?" Georgia said. "He's beautiful."

Belle burst into tears then and laid her head on Georgia's shoulder, both of them gazing at their son.

"Oliver?" Georgia said. They'd considered a few names, but Oliver seemed to be their front-runner.

Belle nodded. "Oliver James."

They both kissed him, and said, "Hello, Oliver James," at the same time.

Belle gazed at Georgia. "You did so well."

"Thank you." She kissed Belle again. "For everything."

By now the midwives and doctors were busy with the placenta delivery down one end, and helping Georgia breastfeed up the other end, so Belle stepped out to ring their parents, and invite them to meet their newest grandchild, or, in the case of Georgia's mum, her only grandchild. Belle also called Tash to let her know to tell the girls they had another new sibling—a brother this time. After the family had all left, Belle and Georgia had some quiet time together, gazing over Oliver and cuddling him. "They sure love him." Georgia smiled at Oliver. "Mum was crying before she even walked into the room."

"Her first grandchild, though. That's to be expected."

"True. She'll get to know the girls in time, too, and then she'll be granny to three."

Belle smiled. It was nice to hear Georgia say that. "And Mum and Dad were thrilled. Their first grandson. I think they're pretty chuffed with him."

"I thought for sure it would be a girl."

Belle shrugged. "You kept changing your mind," she reminded her.

"True, I did. Wow, a son. I really didn't care either way, but he's perfect."

Belle nodded, and the two of them had tears in their eyes.

"He really is perfect, and you were amazing. Actually, I have something for you," Belle said, and rummaged through her bag.

"You've already given me everything I'll ever need," Georgia said, gazing down at Oliver in her arms.

"This is a present, and you can never say no to a present. And don't say Oliver is your present." Belle smiled.

"But he's the best present I ever got…"

"He is, but I wanted to get you something for pushing him out." Belle handed Georgia a small, wrapped box. "A push present."

"Ooh, I did hear about push presents." Georgia looked excitedly at the parcel. She then quickly unwrapped the gift—a gorgeous sapphire ring with small diamonds around it. "Oh my gosh," she said, tears in her eyes. "I've always loved sapphires."

"I know," Belle said, nodding.

"I told you?" Georgia looked confused, and then realised. "Oh, of course, your earrings. Gosh, aren't you clever?" She looked down at her ring as she placed it on her right hand. "I love it," she said, grinning at Belle, "and I love you."

"I hate to ruin this little party," the midwife said as she barged into the room, "but I'm here to check if you wanted to go home tomorrow morning, to have Christmas Day at home, or if you'd rather stay a bit longer, being a first-time mum. Completely your decision."

Georgia nodded, "I'm a first-time mum, but Oliver's other mum has plenty of experience."

The midwife agreed, and Belle blushed, shaking her head. "Every baby's different. I'm not the expert here."

"But you'll know when to call us, if you need to. And we'll do a home visit. Not tomorrow, and not Boxing Day, but maybe on the twenty-seventh?" the midwife said. Being home for Christmas would be nice, Georgia and Belle agreed.

*

TASH AND EMILY dropped into the hospital, with Cora, Ada, and Sophia. At ten weeks old, Sophia looked huge compared to Oliver. "You forget how quickly they grow," Tash said. "I still think of Sophia as my little baby, but next to Oliver, she's a giant." They took some photos of the two girls with Oliver, and then the four children together. Finally, they snapped some pictures of Sophia and Oliver next to one another. Tash was holding Oliver when she turned to Belle. "He looks just like Cora did when she was born." She smiled.

Belle agreed. "I thought so too."

"I can see some similarities across the four kids, actually," Georgia said. "But he has darker hair. Sophia's hair is so light."

"The donor has fairer hair, and of course Emily has blonde hair too," Tash said, nodding. "There's a different genetic mix. But Cora had really dark hair when she was born; it's lightened over the years."

Belle wondered if Tash talking about the genetic mix of the children might bother Georgia at all, but it didn't seem too. In fact, Georgia seemed intrigued to compare the four children. Belle was a little worried that Georgia would feel like she wasn't a part of it, but she was definitely mother— it was undeniable.

As Tash and Emily gathered the girls to leave, Emily said, "I'm sorry we don't have a gift; we rushed out the door and didn't really want to brave the shops on Christmas Eve. We will buy something for you, though."

"Oh," Georgia brushed the comment away, politely, "absolutely no need to."

"We will, though. We want to buy something for him. Have you got Christmas gifts for him?" Emily's eyes widened as she clearly realised they might not be prepared.

"We do." Georgia smiled. "We thought he might be here, so bought some clothes and toys in advance. Just a few things."

"That's great. Organisation is the key, I'm learning," Emily said.

Belle walked Tash, Emily, and the children to the car.

"Bye-bye. You make sure you go to bed early so Santa can come," she said as she kissed her daughters farewell. Their excited grins were lovely to see.

Chapter Twenty-Seven

CHRISTMAS DAY WAS unusual. Instead of waking up and rushing to the tree with the girls, or waking up at her parents' house, Belle woke on the hard couch at the hospital at about 5:00 a.m. She glanced over at Georgia, who was snoring in her hospital bed. Oliver was asleep. He'd last woken at three. Belle rolled back asleep and gently woke to the sound of Oliver's cries. She looked at her watch. It was 5:17 a.m. She'd gotten seventeen more minutes of sleep. *Oh well,* she thought. *I'll take anything I can get for now.* She'd forgotten how broken sleep was with a newborn and how exhausting it was, but also how little bits of sleep here or there would help. And, it was only day one, she reminded herself.

"I feel like I've barely slept," Georgia said. "I think I got all of about three hours."

"It's really hard, but we'll get through it together. And it doesn't feel like it now, in the thick of it, but it gets better."

"Good. I hope it gets better soon." Georgia placed Oliver on her breast. "Hopefully tonight."

"Actually night one is much better than nights two and three."

"Don't tell me that." She shook her head. "I can't handle it. I'll run away and join the circus." She laughed at herself. "Oh wow, listen to me complain. It's taken me forever to get to this point, and here I am complaining on day two."

"It's okay to complain. We'll both complain. Parenting can be sucky, but that doesn't mean you don't want it, don't appreciate it, or don't love him."

"Thanks." Georgia smiled. "It's like you understand what's going on in here." She gestured to her head.

"No, this is something all mums feel, I think."

Georgia smiled at Belle again and reached out to hold her hand. "I can't believe we're doing this together."

"Happy Christmas, Georgia," Belle said.

*

THEY SPENT CHRISTMAS Day at Jo's house, and Belle's parents came over. Alex and Anton dropped in briefly, on their way to Anton's parents' house for lunch. Nikki and Jason came for afternoon drinks and to meet the baby. Belle was thrilled that Georgia's family were so welcoming of her friends and family. With both families present, there was no shortage of people queuing to hold Oliver. Belle and Georgia briefly fell asleep on the couch, taking advantage of all the helping hands around them. They were exhausted, but the day was joyful, with plenty of food and good company. The two families seemed to get along well.

Belle always lost track of time on the days between Christmas and New Year's Eve, but it was particularly bad, in the newborn daze. Sometime in that week, she was standing in the kitchen, making toast for the girls, when Georgia came in. "Can I please have your autograph?" she said as she thrust papers and a pen under Belle's nose.

"Autograph? What for?" Belle asked, squinting at the documents.

"Birth certificate paperwork." Georgia grinned.

"Are you sure?" Although they'd agreed Belle was Oliver's 'other mother,' and they were a couple, Belle had made no assumptions about the legal side of things. That was up to Georgia to work through. She'd assumed, wrongly, obviously, that they'd leave Georgia as a solo mum on Oliver's birth certificate, and then over time change it if their relationship went well—they were such a new couple, after all. "You don't want to wait?"

"Belle, you change his nappies; you sit with us in the middle of the night. You bath him, you dress him, and you're as exhausted as me. You're his mother, 100 per cent. I love you, and you love me. We're here, together. What's the point in waiting?"

Belle kissed Georgia on the forehead. "In that case," she said as she picked up the pen, and then signed her name under Georgia's, with a flourish. Before handing back the documents, she noticed Georgia had given Oliver a hyphenated surname. "Oliver Andrews-Reid," she said out loud. "I like it."

"Me too," Georgia said. "It has a real ring to it."

Epilogue

"STAND OVER THERE," the photographer called out to Belle. "Just move that way." Belle shifted to the left. The photographer looked at the group critically. Gosh, he couldn't have been more than about twenty, Belle thought, and incredibly hip standing there in his skinny jeans and sneakers. He looked really arty—she'd tracked him down through her work. Belle suddenly felt old and dowdy in her baggy white shirt and jeans, but that was the look Tash had insisted on—everyone in white shirts and blue jeans. At least they all had edgy red sneakers on—even the babies—

so that was a bit of a colour pop.

"Okay, now, adults, put your arms around one another if you can. Move that baby to the right a little."

Georgia shifted Oliver a little, and he was now snuggled in between his two mothers. Belle stole a glance at Tash and Emily on the other side, and they had Sophia positioned in a similar way. Tash had bought both babies white shirts and jeans that looked so cute on them. Belle grinned and looked at the camera just in time, as the photographer started to snap. "Everyone turn your head and look at the bigger girls." Everyone looked adoringly at Cora and Ada who were seated in the middle of the photo.

"Now, are you happy to have the girls hold the babies, or prefer not?" The girls were already seasoned at holding their siblings, so Cora held Oliver and Ada held Sophia. The photographer snapped photos of the four siblings together, and then got the two couples to join in the photos too.

"And I think that's a wrap," he said. "Come look."

Tash and Belle made their way to the back of the camera, where he flicked through a few photographs. "I love this one," he said, gesturing to one where the two girls were holding the babies, and the four mothers were crouched down around them. He'd captured the shot really tightly, and everyone looked really happy, with beaming smiles.

"You did a great job," Tash said. Belle was relieved she was happy—the whole photo shoot was her idea, but Belle had organised the photographer, and was a little worried it wouldn't be exactly right for Tash's tastes.

As the photographer busied himself packing away his equipment, Tash nodded toward Emily and Georgia standing talking, holding their babies and clearly sharing stories of parenting. "We did pretty well in the end, didn't we? After all, to be here…at this point in our lives…" Tash said. "We're very lucky."

Belle nodded and grinned. "Modern family, I think."

Tash gave her a big smile and then hugged her friend.

Acknowledgements

I wrote the first draft of *Baby Steps* in 2020, in one of the first lockdowns during COVID-19, staying up on weekend nights as my children slept. Writing this novel became my entertainment, and I really enjoyed getting to know the characters of Belle, Georgia, and Tash throughout the process. I hope you've enjoyed the story too.

Writing a novel is both a solo exercise and one that requires considerable support, so there are always many people to thank.

I'd like to thank my family: My children, who are always happy to chat about my characters with me, for constant support and keeping me grounded at all times. I've become a much better time manager because of you too. This book is dedicated to you. My parents, who instilled a love of reading and writing in me and have always supported me in all facets of life. My supportive sisters, Melanie and Larissa, who are always happy to chat books, plot lines, and characters with me. My author sister, Larissa Johns, is almost always my "first reader," and she was for this one too. Thanks, Larissa, I very much appreciate your constant support and enjoy sharing our writing journeys together.

Thanks also to those around me who support me.

In particular, I'd like to thank Lyssa for being a huge support in all aspects of my life—I often say I think she's my biggest fan, telling everyone who'll listen about my books. I truly appreciate her constant support.

My friends and extended family, thank you for everything. And to all my readers, I thank you for all your support and encouragement.

This story features themes of co-parenting after a breakup. When I wrote *Baby Steps*, I hadn't experienced a breakup with children and tried to imagine what post-breakup co-parenting might be like; my imagination fuelled with stories of my many friends who had been through it, and all the stories and research I've read over the years. Since writing this, I have now personally experienced a broken relationship with my children's other mother, and although it's early days in our co-parenting journey, I think my vision was somewhat realistic, despite the fictional account that is not intended to be representative of my own situation.

I couldn't have done this without my publisher, NineStar Press. Special thanks go to Raevyn McCann and BJ Toth in particular, for all your work on the manuscript and support in getting this book to publication, and to the NineStar Press editing team. Always a joy working with you all. Apologies for my overuse of exclamation marks! I appreciate all your work.

The IVF process is a challenging time for many, and though this book is a lighter romance, I understand it may bring up many emotions for those struggling with fertility. I would encourage you to debrief with someone and wish you all the best in your journey. As soon as I began writing an IVF nurse as a minor character in the book, I knew I'd name her Stella, after the fabulous Irish nurse I had during my IVF experience. IVF can feel long, lonely, and emotional, but the caring nurses really do make a lot of difference, so a special thank-you goes to all my readers who work in carer roles.

I always love to connect with readers and look forward to hearing from you, so please feel free to get in touch and happy reading.

About Gemma Johns

Gemma Johns is the author of four other novels, *The Marriage Sabbatical*, *Similar Features*, *Shaken Worlds*, and *Date at Eight*. She is a professor, fiction writer, and mother. Gemma is never without a notepad and pen, and whenever she gets a spare moment, she is often lost in her head, thinking about the characters she's writing about. This is especially the case when she's hanging the clothes on the clothesline, for some reason. Whenever she can find some down time, Gemma can be found reading, writing, cooking, walking, travelling, or catching up with family and friends. She's a huge fan of podcasts and audiobooks for listening on the go.

Email
gemmajohnsauthor@gmail.com

Facebook
www.facebook.com/profile.php?id=100063466415504

Instagram
www.instagram.com/gemmajohnsauthor

Other NineStar books by this author

Shaken Worlds

Connect with NineStar Press

WWW.NINESTARPRESS.COM

WWW.FACEBOOK.COM/NINESTARPRESS

WWW.FACEBOOK.COM/GROUPS/NineStarNiche

WWW.TWITTER.COM/NINESTARPRESS

WWW.INSTAGRAM.COM/NINESTARPRESS